Layers of Deceit

RODERIC JEFFRIES

Layers of Deceit

An Inspector Alvarez novel

St. Martin's Press
New York

Library of Congress Cataloging in Publication Data

Ashford, Jeffrey, 1926–
 Layers of deceit.

 I. Title.
PR6060.E43L3   1985   823′.914   85-11735
ISBN 0-312-47471-3

First published in Great Britain by William Collins Sons & Co. Ltd.

First U.S. Edition

10 9 8 7 6 5 4 3 2 1

Layers of Deceit

CHAPTER 1

Snow covered the mountains: it had fallen on the roofs of the village houses and even settled on the land: in a visual paradox, it lay on the ripened fruit of orange and lemon trees.

The clouds had finally been blown away and now the sun shone to lend sparkle to the snow. 'Isn't it beautiful?' said Amelia, from her wheelchair.

'For my money, the only time snow's beautiful is on Christmas cards,' replied Hollingborne, six foot four and with a ramrod-straight back.

'How can you be so prosaic?'

'Because I like to be warm.'

Eve Hollingborne laughed. 'Surely you know by now that Tony prefers the pleasures of the flesh to those of the soul?'

'If I wanted snow, I'd go and live in Switzerland,' said Hollingborne, in his sharp-toned voice which so often tended to make a statement a challenge.

'There's not much fear of that unless the firm doubles your pension. Anne was saying only the other evening that she reckons the cost of living in Geneva is twice what it is here.'

'My God, twice!' exclaimed Hart, Amelia's husband. 'And we couldn't afford to live here except for Steve lending us the house and car.' He looked at his watch. 'We'd better get moving or it'll be supper-time before we've had lunch.'

'And I'm hungry!' Amelia smiled at the Hollingbornes. 'Thanks so much. It's always such fun coming here.' She spoke in a way that made it quite clear her words were not mere social conventions. She possessed a genuineness that was unmistakable and people who met her and were initially inclined to be friendly out of sympathy for her infirmity soon discovered a different basis for their relationship because she offered them something that was relatively rare—a warm, undemanding understanding. Friendships among the expatriates of Llueso, as in most such small communities, tended to be of the back-stabbing variety.

She moved her wheelchair forward until the front wheels were just short of the three steps. 'Are you ready, Pat?'

He came forward to take hold of the back of the wheelchair. 'OK to move?'

'I'm holding on . . . If you let go, d'you think I'll toboggan all the way down?'

'I suggest we don't try and find out.' He tilted the chair until the front lifted and the weight came on the back wheels, then let the back wheels ride down one step. 'Are you still all right?'

'Fine. As I said to Carol when she asked me why I didn't have one of those new electric chairs which climbs up and down stairs and does all sorts of other things, I'm much better off with you. You can't short-circuit.'

'The trouble with her is, she's never learned to think as well as talk,' said Eve, annoyed that Carol, a very wealthy woman, should have been so tactless as to ask such a question of the Harts who were obviously not very well off.

Hart moved the wheelchair down the second step, then the third. This brought it to a turning-circle of level land and he let go. 'You're on your own.'

Amelia used one wheel to swing the chair round until she could look to the south. 'It really is gorgeous with all the snow.'

The Hollingbornes' house was almost at the top of the mountainside urbanización and from it there was a view across six kilometres of flat land to the mountain-ringed bay, now even bluer than usual because of the contrast offered by the snow.

'I'd still prefer it to be warm,' said Hollingborne.

She laughed. 'You're just an unrepentant Philistine.'

'Why else d'you think I was in the Ministry of Arts?'

Hart opened the passenger door of the Panda and Amelia manœuvred the wheelchair until it was alongside the doorway, at a slightly inclined angle. He applied the brakes. 'Now I'm wedging the wheel.' He jammed the toe of his right shoe against the outside back wheel, thus preventing any chance of its moving backwards.

She lifted her legs and moved them until her feet were to the side of the footrest, reached up to gain a hold on the top of the opened door, and hauled herself upright. Hart released the brakes of the wheelchair and drew it back. She lowered herself, still holding on to the door, turning as she did so and pushing backwards so that she settled on the seat. She used her hands to lift her legs into the car. It had been an awkward manœuvre, potentially even a dangerous one, but she insisted on employing it because then she was almost independent.

Hart collapsed the wheelchair into its folded position and lifted it into the rear of the car, whose back seat had been folded flat. 'Do we see you at the Cranfords' on Thursday?' he asked the Hollingbornes.

'You do not,' replied Eve, her tone now sharp. She was still a handsome woman, but over the past few years the lines around her mouth had begun to betray the fact that she could be bitchy.

'No doubt we'll see you somewhere else, then . . . You must come and have drinks at our place.'

'You must come and have a meal,' corrected Amelia, through the opened window. 'You haven't had one with us for weeks and I don't know how many we've had with you.'

'Not enough,' said Eve. She spoke emphatically. She'd never have put it so baldly, even to herself, but to see someone as handicapped as Amelia face the world with such cheerful courage made her ready to count her blessings rather than her frustrations.

Hart climbed into the car and started the engine. He

backed and turned, having to use two locks because the turning circle in front of the garage was, from necessity, a small one. Amelia called out a final goodbye, then they drove out and started down towards the first of the hairpin bends. He said: 'Judging from Eve's reactions to my asking about the Cranfords, she and Sue have had a row as rumour suggested. I wonder if Basil's chasing Sue?'

'I don't suppose he's doing anything of the sort. You've just got a nasty mind.'

'What d'you expect after living out here for four months?'

'It's nearer five.'

'Is it really?' As they approached the tight right-hander, he braked and changed down into first, double de-clutching because this had become second nature even when unnecessary.

'We came out on the twelfth of September and today's the fourth of February.'

'I hadn't really realized we were in February.'

'Time out here just vanishes, doesn't it?'

'Maybe we've reached the speed of light.' He rounded the corner, careful to hug the inside, despite the chips of stone which had flaked off the rock-face, because several French lived in the urbanización and they never seemed decided on which side of the road they drove. 'We're very soon going to have to think about returning, then.'

'Yes, except . . . Did I tell you that the last time I spoke to Steve he said he didn't think his friends were coming out after all?'

'You didn't, but he did.'

'Did he also hint that he might offer us the chance of staying on if we want?'

'No.'

'Suppose he does make the offer—how will you feel about it?'

'More to the point, how will you?' he asked, as they neared the next bend, a left-hander.

'I don't really know. It's wonderful out here, but . . .'

'But what?'

'Don't be annoyed at what I'm going to say?'

'After three of Tony's gins I couldn't be annoyed if I wanted to be.'

'Well, the thing is, this is the third time he's had us out. He lends us the house, a car, won't let us pay for the maid or the gardener . . . It can get quite difficult to go on and on accepting charity.'

'What a load of cod's! It's not charity, it's conscience money.'

'For heaven's sake! He can't help being rich.'

He smiled. 'I suppose it is being a little unfair on him . . . I guess it's just that being married to you, some of the family prejudices have rubbed off on to me.'

'If they have, they didn't originate with me.'

He changed gear and turned into the corner. 'Of course not. As Basil once said—in sheer exasperation, probably—you've got the nature of a saint.'

'The damn fool! You won't ever catch me clutching at martyrdom.'

'You can have saints who aren't martyrs.'

'Stop being so ridiculous.' It was true that since her illness she'd had to fight life much harder than most people, but that made her a fighter, not a saint. It annoyed her when people confused the two.

'You'd love it here when it warmed right up. Especially with the swimming.'

In water, she could still move relatively freely; it gave her the illusion that her legs were still under her command.

They left the corner, travelling at little more than twenty kilometres an hour. For someone who had once enthusiastically rallied, he was now a conservative driver.

'I suppose I'd have to go back sometime, to check our flat's OK . . . You'd be able to cope on your own for a very short time, wouldn't you?'

'Yes, of course. But we could always ask Maurice if he'd like to come out.'

'Again? After all, he's only just returned.'

'Why not? He can't normally get away, not with that brood of a family. I thought you liked him?'

'He's quite amusing when he's not on about money.'

'Wouldn't you be, if you'd six mouths to feed?'

'Maybe.'

'Then stop being so critical.'

'I hear. I obey . . . So we stay on here for the summer?' He accelerated gently away from the corner and changed up into second, then third.

'Aren't you counting your chickens even before the eggs have been laid?'

'I'd say it's pretty certain or he wouldn't have passed on the hint to you about our staying.' He braked for the coming right-hander. The brakes began to grip, then they went slack. 'Christ!'

'What's the matter?'

'The brakes have gone.' They were gaining too much speed, despite being in third, because the coming right-hander was the fiercest of the four corners. He went into neutral, revved, into second. The car slowed, but it was still going too fast. Into neutral again, but when he tried to make first the gears refused to mesh because he'd been a fraction out in matching car and gear speed. On the outside there was a sheer drop, unguarded; on the nearside, a tall rock face. With only a couple of seconds left in which to avert disaster, the instinct was to try to ram the gear home. Experience had taught him to overcome instinct. He held the gear in neutral, revved fiercely, waited until the revs had peaked and were just beginning to die, and then tried again to engage first. The gear slid home.

He pulled on the handbrake and that and first gear began to slow them, but their speed was still too great as he entered the corner and the car began to slide. Using the accelerator, since the car was front-wheel drive, and opposite lock, he regained control, but left the corner quickly.

The road down to the fourth and final bend was not so steep and their speed did not become dangerous. They rounded the corner with a quick squeal of rubber and some body lurch, then there was a straight road, level after a couple of hundred metres. Eventually, the handbrake brought them to a stop.

She reached out and gripped his right hand. 'That was interesting, but I don't think I want to try it again.'

CHAPTER 2

Alvarez turned off the new square—new only in the sense that it was not as old as the one right in the centre of Llueso —and walked along Calle Luis Vives to the garage. In the show window was a gleaming-smart Seat Ronda. A far cry from his ancient Seat 600 which was beginning to arouse the derision of irreverent little boys. He sighed. New Rondas were for the doctors and the foreigners of the world, not the overworked detectives.

He went into the main body of the garage and skirted the pit. Two mechanics were standing round a wrecked VW with German plates. 'Where's Julio?' he asked.

After a moment, the elder mechanic shrugged his shoulders.

A middle-aged man, wearing glasses on a round, pudgy face, his hands oily, came up to Alvarez. 'Magdalena saw Dolores yesterday afternoon and she said she wasn't too fit—nothing serious, I hope?'

'A cold, that's all. But it's a nuisance because it means she may not bother with things as she should.'

'I know. If Magda's got one of her heads, the grub's poor. And that's not funny after a hard day's work.'

They thought about the crosses they had to bear. Finally
Alvarez said: 'I'm looking for Julio.'

'What's the time?'

'Near enough to a quarter to ten.'

'Then he'll have gone off for his breakfast.'

Alvarez's expression brightened. 'I'll go and find him.'

He left the garage, crossed the road and went along to
the Bar Alhambra. Inside, half a dozen men were standing
by the bar and Roselló was one of them.

Roselló was roughly the same age as Alvarez, but his face
was less lined and he looked younger. He said: 'I suppose
you want something?'

'I wouldn't say no to a coñac.'

'I'd bloody faint if you did.'

'A large one.'

'Here, d'you think I'm made of money?'

The man on the far side of Roselló said: 'You must be,
seeing what you charged for working on my car.'

'You try employing half a dozen layabouts and see how
rich you end up. Try to get 'em to do a proper day's work
and they laugh in your face. And you can't sack 'em, not
without paying a fortune.'

'Things aren't like they used to be,' said the barman, as
he pushed a glass across to Alvarez.

Alvarez sipped the brandy. Things had changed beyond
measure, from the moment the Caudillo had died and
democracy had come to Spain. With democracy had come
pornographic films and videos, an ever-growing rate of drug
addiction, an explosion of thefts and muggings, and a young
who refused to learn the oldest of all truths, that in this
world one never got something for nothing . . .

Roselló drained his glass and looked at Alvarez, but sadly
came to the conclusion that he would not be offered the
other half. 'I'd best be getting back. If I'm not there, the
lazy sods stand around, doing nothing.'

Roselló was in far better condition than his corpulent

body suggested and his rate of walking was brisk, so that by the time they reached the garage Alvarez was out of breath. They went past the inspection pit and stopped by a light blue Panda. 'This belongs to an Englishman from Santa Victoria,' said Roselló. 'He's lent it to a cousin who's staying this end of the island. She's in a wheelchair, but as cheerful as they come and hasn't got her nose in the air, like some of the bitches who just shout louder and louder when I can't understand what the hell they're trying to say . . .'

Alvarez listened without impatience to the long, rambling complaint, content to let time slide on towards lunch and those squid, stuffed with sausage and sautéd with onions, tomatoes, dry sherry, and ground cinnamon—always assuming that Dolores had the strength of mind to pull herself together . . .

Roselló finally returned to the matter in hand. 'A couple of days ago we got to pick this car up. She and her husband had been up at one of the top houses in El Cielo and when they were driving down the brakes failed.'

'That's one hell of a place for that to happen!' Alvarez studied the car more closely. 'They must have been near the bottom, or they'd have crashed.'

'The brakes went before the third bend.'

'That's the worst of the lot, isn't it?'

'The wife said her husband used to go in for car rallies. He used the gears and the handbrake to slow them down enough to get round the corner.'

'Sooner him than me.'

'And me.'

Alvarez shook his head. 'Where's my interest in all this?'

'I brought the car back on the end of a solid tow-bar and left it until yesterday evening, on account of having so much other work to do. Then I put it over the pit and checked to see what kind of a job it was going to be . . .' He paused for a moment. 'One of the brake lines was fractured and all the fluid had run out.' He looked up. 'From the look of things, that line could have been deliberately damaged.'

'How sure are you?'

'I'm not. That's why I said "could have been". They live down a dirt track and you know as well as me how stones get thrown up all the time, and there's no knowing where a stone'll end up . . . But if you asked me to come straight out and give an opinion, I'd say it wasn't a stone, it was something like a knife.'

'If it was deliberate, would it have to have been done at the house where they'd been?'

'Not necessarily. If you know what you're doing, you can weaken the line to the point where it'll carry on until you're braking really hard, when it's bound to give.'

'You're saying there was an attempt to kill them?'

'I'm saying there might have been. Have a look for yourself and see what I mean about not being able to be certain.'

Alvarez shook his head. 'It wouldn't mean anything to me.' He rubbed his chin, stubbled because he had forgotten to shave that morning. 'What have you said to 'em—I mean, the people who were in the car?'

'I haven't said anything. I reckoned you'd know what to do.'

'It would be a lot easier if only you could be certain.'

'Well, I can't.'

Alvarez sighed. 'I'd better go and see them, then. I can't just sit back and do nothing after you've told me this.'

'It wouldn't be the first time,' replied Roselló, satisfied that the responsibility was now no longer his.

Ca'n Oñar lay beyond the rolling crest of a hill, to the south-east of the Palma road. In the fields about it were orange and lemon trees, laden with ripe fruit, almond trees curtained in white, or occasionally pink, blossom, and fig trees whose leafless branches, ending in numerous upturned twigs, looked like dead men's fingers. Some fields were newly ploughed or cultivated, others were growing field beans or grass.

As he climbed out of the car, Alvarez noted the small, stone-built building three hundred metres to the right of the house.. Probably this housed a well which tapped a stream or underground lake and would never run dry, even in the hottest and longest of summers. Such a well, before the foreigners had forced prices sky high, had been worth almost as much as the house ... The house was old—perhaps a couple of hundred years—and simple, built by people concerned only with the bare essentials of shelter. Yet for him it was far more attractive than any of the modern, luxurious houses which the foreigners had had built ...

The glass-panelled front door opened and a woman in a wheelchair propelled herself forward and then came to a stop in the middle of the patio, under the bare, pruned branches of two ancient vines which had been trained along wires three metres above the ground. 'Good morning,' she said in Spanish, as he walked across.

He answered in English, introducing himself.

'You're a detective? How terribly interesting!'

He responded to her friendliness and smiled briefly. 'I'm glad of that, señora. Because if you had said, how worrying, I might have begun to wonder why.'

' "Thus conscience doth make cowards of us all." ... But come inside. The wind's quite cold.'

He wondered whether he should help her by pushing the wheelchair into the house, decided she would sooner manage on her own.

'You're quite right,' she said.

He started.

'Whenever I meet people for the first time and Pat's not here, they wonder whether they should give me a hand. It's very kind of them, but I'd infinitely rather do everything for myself.'

After she'd turned the wheelchair, he followed her into the house.

'Will you have coffee or would you prefer a drink?'

'A coñac would be very nice, señora.'

'And I'll have tea. I have to watch my weight, so I restrict myself to one drink a day and one glass of wine with each meal. It's frustrating, living in a country where the drink's so reasonable and not being able to indulge . . . Come on through to the other room.'

Beyond the hall was the sitting-room, oblong and with a high, very simply beamed roof ceiling. The furniture was Spanish and serviceable rather than elegant, there was a gaily patterned carpet on the tiled floor, and four very colourful paintings of local scenes hung on the walls. The stove, in one corner, was wood-fired and logs were stacked to one side of it.

'Do sit down. I won't be a moment.' She propelled the wheelchair to the two-way door at the far end of the sitting-room and used the chair to push it open. The door swung shut behind her.

He was not surprised that Roselló, usually so critical of foreigners, had expressed admiration for her. Already, he was conscious of her bubbling sense of vitality and of a certainty that when she met someone she looked for the good qualities in that person rather than the bad.

When she returned, a tray was balanced across the arms of the wheelchair. 'It's one-o-three. I hope you like that brand?'

'Señora, I like all coñacs.'

She laughed. 'You sound like my husband. There is no such thing as a bad brandy, only one that is better than another.' She moved closer to his chair and held out the glass.

He took the glass from her. 'You health, señora.'

'And I'll drink to yours—that is, if you don't mind being toasted in tea? At home, it's supposed to be an insult to toast anyone in water.'

'We don't have such a custom here.'

'That's not surprising when there's so little need to drink water.' She moved the wheelchair slightly back, used a spoon to knead the slice of lemon in the tea.

'Señora, is your husband here?'

'He isn't, no. Our car broke down and so we've been left without transport. Pat rang the garage this morning, but they said it still wasn't repaired, so he decided to hire a car. Then he rang Steve—that's my cousin who lent us the Panda—to tell him the situation and Steve said we could borrow another car until the Panda is fixed. So Pat's gone to Santa Victoria by bus and I'm afraid I don't know when he'll be back. Presumably you wanted to speak to him?'

'Yes, I did.'

'What's he been up to?'

He smiled. 'Nothing serious, señora! It's to do with your car. The owner of the garage called me this morning to say he'd examined it and was a little worried.'

'In what way worried?'

'The brakes failed because one of the lines had been damaged. He thinks it's possible that the damage might have been done deliberately.'

She frowned. 'Are you suggesting that someone tried to make us crash? Impossible!'

'There's no one you can think of who might try and do a thing like that?'

'Good God, no!'

'You haven't, perhaps, had a serious argument with anyone recently?'

'I haven't and I'm certain Pat hasn't either. In any case, can you imagine an ex-colonial officer from Funafuti or a retired bank manager from Budleigh Salterton doing anything like that?'

'Have you had any problems with staff?'

'Our only staff is Lucía who normally comes five days a week to do the housework, but is usually ill once a week on

whichever day her husband's not working at the Parelona
Hotel.'

'Is the car normally kept here?'

'In the garage.'

'And is that locked at night?'

'We didn't bother at first because everything was so
wonderfully quiet and peaceful, but friends told us that
there were a lot of thefts these days and it was advisable to
keep everything locked.'

'I'm afraid that's true, señora. Ten years ago, you could
have left the house unlocked for a month and nothing would
have been touched. Now . . .'

'The tourists have brought you prosperity; but you've had
to pay heavily for it.'

He was warmed by her understanding. 'Indeed we have.'

'And you can't turn the clock back.'

He left ten minutes later and she accompanied him to the
front door. Just before opening the door, he said: 'Perhaps
you would ask your husband to telephone me at the post—
I will write the number down—to tell me if he can suggest
anyone who might have sabotaged the car?'

'Of course I'll do that. But I can tell you the answer
now—there's no one.'

The telephone rang, jerking Alvarez awake. He opened his
eyes and blearily stared resentfully at his watch. Half past
three. What moron was telephoning during siesta time?

'This is Patrick Hart. My wife said you wanted me to get
in touch. As she told you, it's quite impossible that anyone
could have sabotaged the car.'

'You've not recently had an argument with anyone, either
a foreigner or a Mallorquin?'

'Not the kind that would end up in attempted murder—
because that's what you're suggesting, isn't it?'

'Yes, señor.'

'No, the brake failure was an accident: just one of those

unfortunate things that can happen with a car.'

'Then now I can be certain. Thank you for calling, señor.'

Alvarez replaced the receiver. Despite Roselló's reservations, the fracture in the brake line had been caused by a stone. He settled more comfortably in the chair. Dolores had managed to pull herself together and the meal had been as good as anticipation had suggested. Filled with contentment, he closed his eyes.

CHAPTER 3

Alan Cullom drew level with the drystone wall, topped with a three-foot-high chain-link fence, which marked the boundary of Ca'n Cullom's land. He dropped his holdall and sat on the edge of the wall, resting his back against the chain-link, even though there were now only a couple of hundred metres to the gates. He took a handkerchief from his jeans and wiped the sweat from his forehead. Late May and the temperatures were already in the mid-eighties. The bus had been packed, someone near him had not had a bath in days, and the heat, despite all the open windows, had been enervating. Then there'd been the long walk from the main road to Santa Victoria, built on and around a hill, and the longer walk out from there to Ca'n Cullom. (Castle Howard was named after the Howard family, so Steve had renamed his castle in the sun. Unfortunately, he hadn't done this in a spirit of mocking fun.)

Alan stood, picked up the holdall, and carried on to the large and elaborately designed wrought-iron gates, which were shut. On each gate was a notice, featuring a snarling dog's head and the message, in English and in Spanish, that at night the house and grounds were guarded by a fierce dog. Karl Marx. One man's visible ego . . .

He opened the right-hand gate and went in: the gate shut

with a ringing sound. He began to walk up the loose-chip drive towards the line of oleander bushes which marked the brow of the hill. A woman's voice, muffled, reached him. 'Come here. Karl. Sit. Will you come back . . .' She whistled.

He stopped and waited. A large, black, wavy-haired dog appeared, bounding over the grass. As it neared him, it slowed to a walk and began to growl and its lips drew back to show a vicious set of fangs.

'Whoever you are, just stand still. He won't hurt you,' shouted the woman.

'You hear that, you stupid black bastard?' said Alan.

The dog came to a halt. Hair practically obscured its eyes, nevertheless it did seem as if there were now an expression of indecision on its broad face. It stopped snarling.

'Are you so thick you've completely forgotten me?'

The dog wagged its stump of a tail, but did not move.

'Karl, Karl,' the woman called out desperately.

Alan Cullom said to the dog: 'And according to Steve, you're totally obedient . . . Come and say hullo.' He patted his leg. The dog took two steps forward, stopped. 'You poor old sod—you don't know whether to greet me or to eat me, do you?' The dog again wagged its stumpy tail. 'Silly bastard!' he said, meaning his brother. The first time he'd come here after Karl Marx had been imported from England, Steven had told him about the superbly trained, incredibly fierce guard dog he'd just bought; at one word of command, it would corner any intruder; it treated every stranger as hostile until ordered to do otherwise . . . They'd gone round to the kennels to see this canine wonder, but not before Steven had warned him not to get too close to the chained dog or he'd be savagely attacked . . . He'd always had a sympathetic understanding with dogs. It had, therefore, seemed a perfectly natural thing to do to walk straight up to the dog, despite Steven's panicky shout to get back, and let it sniff him and, the introductions over, make friends. Karl had begun to make friends. And Steven, who'd always lacked any sense of humour when he'd thought he might have been made to look a bit of a fool, had been furious . . . From then on, Steven had tried to set Karl against him and now the bewildered dog didn't know whether to obey his instincts or his training . . .

The woman came running up. 'I'm terribly sorry . . . Are you all right?'

'Quite intact.'

Sweating heavily, breathing quickly, she came to a halt. She stared at him, then at Karl, and her expression became more perplexed than worried. 'He hasn't gone for you at all?'

'No.'

'When I heard the gate and he took off, I ran as fast as I could. I kept shouting to him to come back.'

'I heard you.'

'I was terrified he'd attack you.'

'Karl has rightly retained a sneaking sympathy for the lumpen proletariat.'

'How d'you know his name? Who are you?'

'I suppose I could put the same question to you.'

She used her hand to brush a shallow curl of hair away from her forehead. 'Will you please tell me who you are?'

She looked very different, he thought, from the woman who'd been here six months back. That one had been tarted right up and so certain that she was going to become mistress of the house that she'd begun to understudy the part. Steven had got rid of her efficiently and with a minimum of fuss. But this woman wasn't in the least obvious. Her jeans weren't so tight that imagination became unnecessary and it had been fairly obvious, when she'd been running, that she was wearing a brassière under her cotton shirt. Slightly older than Steven normally liked, she had an open face, a snub nose, whimsical eyebrows, and curly, corn-coloured hair now in some disarray. 'My name's

Alan,' he said. 'I'm looking for a bed.'

'Are you expected?'

'No.'

'Then . . .' She stopped, became confused. 'You don't mean you're Steve's brother?'

'Don't you see any family likeness?'

'But you're so much younger.'

'My father's second marriage was late, but enthusiastic.'

'You could have said who you were at the beginning and saved me making a bit of a fool of myself.'

'I apologize humbly.'

She looked at him, uncertain, worried.

'Is it all right if we carry on to the house? I've been dreaming of a very cold, very long gin and tonic for the past hour and a quarter and I don't think I can stand much more frustration, even in the name of good manners.'

'There's no need . . . I was only trying to prevent you being hurt.'

'And for that, I thank you.' He began to walk. Karl watched him for a few seconds, then followed, keeping on the grass, obviously still unable to decide whether to be friendly, or not.

When he reached the line of oleanders, the view and the house came into sight. The land sloped away, except for a level area on which the house stood, and the whole of the central plain of the island was visible together with Playa Nueva Bay, the mountains which backed it, and the sea beyond. The land was not yet dried up and there were endless shades of green to contrast the blues of the sea and sky. A couple of restored windmills were just visible, their coloured wooden sails turning lazily in the slight breeze as they pumped water. A man of imagination saw Don Quixote advancing to do battle . . . Steven had little imagination. He'd not bought the house because of its setting, but because it was of such a size and quality that it was obvious only a rich man could ever have afforded it.

He spoke to her. 'D'you realize you haven't yet told me your name?'

She didn't answer immediately and he thought she was going to ignore him, but then she said: 'Susan. Susan Pride.'

'And where's Steve? Stretched out by the pool, carefully cultivating that bronzed jet-set look?'

'He's in Palma.'

'Doing what?'

'I've no idea.'

They reached the house. He opened the right-hand panelled front door, with its small inspection port protected by a grille, and stood aside to let her enter first. Then he said to Karl: 'Well, how about you?'

'Steve doesn't like him in the house,' she said.

'I know,' he answered, as he dropped the holdall and finally shut the door when it was clear Karl was not entering. 'According to the experts, dogs carry around with them all sorts of horrible diseases which they sometimes pass on to humans and Steve has only to read about a disease to suffer from it.'

'Do you . . .' She stopped.

'Do I what?'

She lifted her head slightly, making it more evident that her chin was a determined one. 'Are you always so sarcastic about the people who try to help you?'

'To be helped is to be resentful. And in any case, when Steve helps his motive isn't all that altruistic; it makes him feel very righteous to give a crust of bread to his beachcombing brother.'

'That's a pretty cheap thing to say.'

'I'm cut-price by nature . . . I now require one gin and tonic as a life-saver, one as a restorative, and one for pleasure. Joining me?'

'You'll be beastly about him, but drink his gin?'

'In my state of thirst, I'll drink anybody's gin.'

She crossed the hall to the stairs and went up them to the

half-landing, continued up and out of sight. He entered the sitting-room, very large, with picture windows along the south wall giving the view across to the sea. It could have been an attractive room, but Steven had brought together too much furniture and furnishings that were ostentatiously good; it looked like an exhibition room, badly mounted and without taste.

The mobile cocktail cabinet was against the far wall and a quick check showed that the ice-bucket was empty. He carried this through to the kitchen. A small, plump woman with a noticeable scar on her right cheek was peeling potatoes. When she saw him, she gave a cry of delight, dropped potato and peeler, and hurried to embrace him. He grinned. It was a pity Steven wasn't there to see this. Steven did not believe in familiarity between employer and employee. That was one of the reasons why many Mallorquins regarded him with amusement.

María wanted to know how he was, where he'd been, what he'd been doing, and how long was he going to stay? And, she continued almost in the same breath, wasn't it just like him to turn up when she was preparing a truly delicious lunch for the señorita? Had he smelled the cooking? He answered in his easy, if frequently ungrammatical, Spanish that for weeks he'd been dreaming of her cooking. Then he filled the ice-bucket from the ice-making machine and returned to the sitting-room.

He drank his first gin and tonic. When the glass was empty, he decided to leave the next drink until he'd washed. He went into the hall, picked up the holdall, and climbed the stairs.

There was an oblong landing, off which led five bedrooms, each with bathroom en suite. The master bedroom, very large and with two dressing-rooms, was immediately opposite the head of the stairs while to the left of this was the main guest room; the three remaining bedrooms faced north and were on the other side of the landing. He crossed to the door of the main guest bedroom, opened it, and stepped inside.

Susan had taken off her jeans and shirt and was lying on top of the further bed, wearing a red and black brassière and bikini pants. For a moment she was too surprised to react, then she sat up. 'Would you mind getting out of my room?'

'But aren't you . . .' He stopped. 'Look, I'm sorry. But normally when no one else is staying here I use this room.'

'And you'd already managed to forget that I was staying here?'

'It's just that I thought . . .' Again, he stopped.

'D'you mind getting out?' There was more than anger in her voice now.

He left. She presented an odd mixture of character, he thought. It was almost as if she'd been embarrassed by his logical assumption that she was sharing Steven's bed.

Being on the south-east slope, Ca'n Cullom lost the sun in the early part of the evening. In summer, there was a sharp change of light when the sun became hidden and then a slow deepening of twilight; for those who liked gentle peace, this was the most beautiful part of the day. Steven Cullom returned home as twilight was finally merging into darkness.

Typically, he drove a very expensive car, a blood red Ferrari Boxer, even though it could not have been more unsuitable on the restricted roads of the island. He left it in the garage, went through the utility room to the kitchen where he met his brother. 'You're here! When did you arrive?'

'In time for one of María's masterpieces.'

They were half-brothers, but both in character and physically they had little in common. Steven respected wealth, position, and the approval of others; Alan seemed to reject wealth and position, and, by his open disregard for others' opinions, deliberately to court their disapproval. Steven, at

47, was a tall, large, heavily featured man, beginning to become flabby; Alan, at 28, was taller, hard and lean, and slightly battered-looking. A casual acquaintance might have described Steven as serious and solid, Alan as irresponsible; someone who knew them better would have added the hint of weakness in Steven's character, the evidence of hardness in Alan's. In a position of difficulty, Steven would always seek to escape by guile, Alan by strength. Both men instinctively recognized this. It amused Alan, but it was a source of irritation to Steven.

Steven ran the palm of his hand over his rapidly thinning hair. 'I'd have liked some warning . . . Why didn't you let me know?'

'Because I didn't know I was coming.'

He controlled his irritation which experience had taught him merely led to his looking pompous when matched against his brother's irreverent mockery. 'You must have had some warning?' He crossed to the large refrigerator and opened the right-hand door to bring out a bottle of Codorniu Extra.

'No one knew anything was wrong until the owner discovered he'd been swindled by the last charterer. By then, his cheques were bouncing left, right, and centre and before he'd time to draw breath a court order was slapped on the yacht and we couldn't escape to sea. So that was that. I managed to work a passage on a yacht which was sailing from Cannes to here, much to your good luck or I'd have had to wire for funds.'

'I told you from the first that that job was no good.'

'True. But unfortunately you didn't go on to suggest an alternative and, frankly, at the time I was beginning to get the impression that I might have overstayed my welcome.'

Steven didn't deny that. Like so many wealthy people, he was very quick to decide someone was trying to live at his expense, more especially when that someone was a relative. He gestured with the bottle. 'You've met Susan?'

'Of course.'

'D'you know where she is right now?'

'The last time I saw her she was still out on the patio, braving the mosquitoes.'

Steven walked past Alan. 'Will you bring three glasses with you? Tulip ones.'

'You're not using tumblers any longer?' It was a childish remark, but there were times when Steven managed to irritate Alan. Strangely, it was almost always when he'd not had any intention of doing so.

Alan only heard the sound because he had, unknowingly, left the door of the bedroom unlatched and a slight draught had opened it a little. He laid the book down on the bed and looked up. The sound was twice repeated.

He climbed out of bed, crossed to the door and opened it wide. Steven stood in front of the door of Susan's bedroom, one hand on the handle, the other raised to knock again. He suddenly realized he was being watched and dropped his hand.

'*Pas çe soir, Joséphine?*' said Alan.

Steven, face flushed, left and went along and into his own room. Alan closed the door, making certain that this time it clicked firmly shut, and climbed back into bed. The fact that Steven had been knocking suggested that Susan had locked the door, which in turned suggested that she'd not yet granted him her favours. Why not?

Alan laughed aloud. Steve—who'd always had the desires of a randy billygoat—had recently had the money to follow up his fancies and he'd bedded any number of strikingly beautiful women. It was ironic that now he should be denied by one who, though perhaps piquantly attractive, was certainly no beauty. Very frustrating for him.

CHAPTER 4

Alvarez parked his car, crossed the pavement, and went along the narrow covered passage to the small patio outside the kitchen. As he came abreast of one of the three orange trees planted there, one of Juan's and Isabel's canaries began to sing. He looked up at the cage, suspended from a bracket to keep it clear of maruading cats, and smiled. If a canary sang when it first saw you, that meant good luck.

He pushed through the bead curtain into the kitchen. Dolores, wearing an apron over a brightly coloured cotton frock, was by the stove, stirring the contents of a large saucepan. 'That smells delicious. What is it?'

She leant the wooden spoon against the side of the saucepan, turned, put her hands on her hips, and regarded him. 'Always the first question! What's to eat? Never, how am I, is my headache still agonizingly painful!'

Damnit, but a man never knew what to say. Usually, she was delighted to be asked what she was cooking. 'I'm sorry, I didn't know you had a bad head.'

'I haven't.'

'But you've just said . . .'

'If I had had the most blinding of headaches, all that would concern you would be what was for the next meal.' Her deep, musical voice was thick with scorn; her head was held high and her expression was haughty; she looked like a cantante flamenca communing with her soul.

'I'm sorry,' he mumbled, uncertain about what he was apologizing. He hurried through to the dining-room. Jaime was seated at the table in front of a bottle of brandy and two glasses. His expression was glum. Alvarez sat opposite him, reached across for a glass, and poured himself a very generous brandy. 'Is there any ice?'

'In the refrigerator.'

Alvarez turned and looked at the doorway. To reach the refrigerator it would be necessary to cross the kitchen. He drank, then said: 'What's up with her?'

'How would I know? She was all right this morning when I left . . . But when I came back, five minutes ago, and asked what was for grub, she blew up like a volcano.'

'She went for me for not asking how her headache was. Then when I did ask about it, she said she hadn't got one.' He finished the brandy. 'D'you think she's going a bit crazy, like some women do?'

'God knows!'

'You'd better do something about it if she is.'

'What?'

That was a good question. Spanish women still knew their place in life and normally observed it, rightly accepting unconditionally any criticisms their husbands were called upon to make. But Dolores was . . . different. And it was always best not to upset her . . .

The front door was opened and then slammed shut. The two children rushed into the room. 'I'm starving,' Juan announced loudly. 'What's for lunch?'

'Who knows?' answered Jaime.

'I'll go and ask Mum . . .'

'You stay here.'

'Why?'

'It's safer, that's why. She's in one of her—' He hastily stopped as Dolores appeared in the kitchen doorway.

'I am what?' she asked casually, as if the answer were of little account.

Jaime mumbled something.

She turned to the children. 'Juan, have you washed your hands?'

'They're not dirty.'

'Stop arguing. Upstairs and wash them. Isabel, lay the table—that is, if you can persuade your father and your uncle to move away from the bottle for long enough. And hurry, both of you, because you're late and the meal is probably already ruined.'

Lunch, despite the fact that the bacalao a la vizcaína turned out to be delicious, was a sombre meal. And the moment they'd finished the bananas and baked almonds, Dolores told the children to go out and play.

Normally, being a precocious eleven-year-old, Juan would have argued that he wanted to stay in. But he had learned when it was necessary to do as he was told. He left, followed by his sister.

Alvarez said: 'And I'd better be moving. I've a lot of work . . .'

'Sit down,' she ordered.

He sat. He poured himself another brandy.

'Sofía phoned this morning,' she said. 'She told me about Cousin Inés.' Her voice and expression changed and suddenly it was obvious that she was very troubled. 'You remember Cousin Inés?'

Alvarez tried to recall her, but failed. On the island family ties were strong and there were so many 'cousins' that for a man it was impossible to identify them all.

'She lives near Palma Nova and has two sons and a daughter. They came to Fernandez's wedding two years back and you and Jaime couldn't keep your eyes off Beatriz, the daughter.'

'D'you mean that girl with beautiful black hair who looked like . . .' He stopped. It was difficult for a middle-aged man to describe a young naiad without sounding either lustful or ridiculous.

'She . . .' Dolores's face crumpled and she began to cry.

Jaime stared at her with concern, then reached across the table; she gripped his hand. She was a woman of sharp emotions: when she was happy, she was on a cloud; when she was sad, her whole world wept.

'What has happened to Beatriz?' Alvarez asked.

'She . . . she tried to commit suicide.'

They were shocked. They were of an age for the act of suicide to be a sin of terrifying magnitude; that a relation of theirs should have attempted it left them feeling as if they were partially to blame.

'Why?' asked Alvarez.

'She won't say. She cut her wrists with a knife, but missed the arteries. She won't tell her mother or anyone why she did it and Inés is going out of her mind with worry. Enrique, you know how to get people to tell you things. Go and see Beatriz and find out what happened.'

The bay of Palma had once been beautiful, but beauty filled no bank balances; the shoreline had been developed and most of the beauty had been submerged under a concrete jungle. Yet, away from the overcrowded beaches, apartment blocks, hotels, memento shops, restaurants, discos, night clubs, and cafés, it was still possible to find a hint of what there had once been. Ca N' Atona stood on rising ground and from the patio one overlooked the developed coastal strip to see the azure bay and the cloudless sky.

Inés had been widowed when Beatriz, the youngest of her three children, had been ten and the financial struggle to bring them up was reflected in her lined, leathered face. Yet, just as with the bay, it was possible to discern the beauty there had once been. She fidgeted with her fingers as she sat at the rough wooden table set out on the patio. 'I've begged and begged her to tell me. But she won't . . . My Beatriz, who has always told me everything.' Tears trickled down her weathered cheeks.

Amadeo, the elder son, who was standing behind her chair, put a hand on her shoulder. Félix, the younger, seated at the table, looked up. 'It was a man,' he said fiercely.

'That's impossible . . .' she began.

'I tell you, it was a man.'

'She couldn't do such a thing.' She turned to Alvarez.

'I've brought her up as a girl should be. So how could she behave like that?'

'Things are often different now,' he replied sadly.

'We'll find who it was,' said Félix, 'and we'll kill him.' He slammed his clenched fist down on the table. His father had been born in Jerez de la Frontera and in him ran the fiery, romantic, irrational passions of the Andalucian character.

'It's best not to talk like that,' said Alvarez.

'I'll talk as I want.' His skin was dark, his hair black, his eyes a very deep brown; touched with the gipsy, the Mallorquins said.

'We don't know . . .' began Amadeo.

'Goddamnit, I know.'

'Félix,' Alvarez said, 'you do not know, you only assume. Which means that without any evidence at all, you're ready to besmirch your sister's honour.'

'You talk like an old fool.'

'Félix!' exclaimed his mother, shocked by such rudeness.

He rose suddenly and went into the house, slamming a door behind him.

'He's always been so fond of Beatriz,' Inés said in a low voice. She looked appealingly at Alvarez. 'Surely he can't be right?'

'I pray to God he isn't.'

'Will you go and see her in hospital?'

'Of course.'

'If . . .' She stopped, swallowed heavily several times, then said in a whisper: 'If she gives you a name, I beg of you, Enrique, don't let Félix know what that name is.'

The clinic stood on the northern outskirts of Palma. Alvarez parked his car, then walked round to the main entrance. He spoke to the assistant director and, after identifying himself, explained that he wanted to talk to Beatriz Bennassar. But before he did so, had anyone in the hospital learned what had led her to try to commit suicide? The assistant director left the office, returning five minutes later to say she had discovered herself to be pregnant. He added that she had begged the hospital not to tell the family and, since she was of age, the request had been strictly observed.

The psychological strain and the physical pain had touched her with a kind of radiance so that when Alvarez first saw her, propped up in one of the two beds in the room, he was shaken by the immediate thought that she looked like the Madonna. He handed her the flowers he'd bought from a stand in La Rambla, in Palma, then sat on the edge of the second bed. Both her wrists were bandaged and she kept touching a bandage with the fingers of her other hand. She was wearing a beautifully embroidered bedjacket which, he guessed, had been made by her mother.

'I've just come from your family.'

She turned her face away.

'Your mother is desperately worried. She's asked me to try to find out what has happened. She's frantic because you won't tell her so she can know how to help.'

She said nothing.

'Wouldn't it be kinder to tell her? After all, she'll have to discover before too long, won't she?'

'They've told you,' she said wildly.

'Yes, they have. But I promise you that no one in your family will ever learn what has happened from me.'

She began to cry.

He moved and sat on her bed and comforted her as he would his own daughter. After a while, she began to calm down and stop crying. 'These days it's not the end of the world,' he said, trying to sound convincing.

'I . . . I was so certain he'd marry me when I told him. But all he said was, I must get an abortion. I told him I couldn't because it was not allowed by the Church. He . . . he . . .' She began to cry once more.

Alvarez could guess what he'd said. If she was that pious,

why had she let him seduce her? Such a man was incapable
of understanding that for a woman love could become so
great that she would even forget her faith, but that it
had only been temporarily forgotten, not denied. 'What
happened when you refused to have an abortion?'

'He said I was stupid and I had to have one. He offered
me a hundred thousand pesetas. When I refused to take the
money, he became angry.'

'Who is he?'

She didn't answer.

'Give me his name. I'll persuade him to help you.'

'No.'

'Why not? Is he already married?'

She shook her head.

She loved him still, he thought, and in her heart there
was the hope that he would return to her. 'Don't you
understand that if he and I talked . . .'

'I won't tell you,' she said fiercely as she jerked herself
free of him.

He stood, crossed to the window, and looked out at the
distant mountains.

'What . . . what's Félix saying?'

He turned. 'Can't you guess?'

'He mustn't ever find out. If he does, he'll do something
terrible . . .'

'Only you know who the father is, so he can do nothing
unless you tell him.'

'I'll never do that,' she said fiercely.

CHAPTER 5

Friday night was still and hot and it might have been
mid-July rather than the end of May. Alan, not yet ready
for sleep, left the house. The moon was full and the sky

cloudless and from the pool patio it was possible to make out the shimmer of the distant sea. Cicadas were shrilling, a Scops owl was belling, and just audible was the unmusical, but not unpleasant, clanging of sheep's bells.

He walked down the steps at the side of the pool patio and across the sloping lawn of gama-grass to the first drystone wall of the terracing. He sat. He wondered how long it had originally taken to fashion the terraces and how poor the economy must have been to make it worth while to invest so much time and labour to bring under difficult cultivation so little land. Near him there grew an ancient olive tree. In the moonlight, its twisted, hollow main trunk looked tortured. It was one of the few now remaining. When Steven had bought the property, he'd employed a consultant landscape architect whose brief had been to design a garden more striking than any other on the island. The man, who had had considerable expert knowledge but no instinctive love of natural beauty, had decided to fill the terraces with a profusion of unusual flowers, shrubs, and trees, and in consequence he'd had almost all the olives and almonds ripped out. The terraces were now exotically striking, but they no longer belonged.

There was a sound from somewhere behind and Alan turned; in the moonlight he could just make out Susan as she descended the steps by the side of the pool. He was sorry she was approaching. Recognizing how easily he could like her a lot, he'd been careful during the past few days to make certain they were seldom on their own together. Whatever her true relationship with Steven, there was no future in one developing between himself and her.

'Alan. Where are you?'

Since she'd obviously seen him cross the lawn, there was no point in remaining silent. He called out. She half turned and came directly over to where he was seated. She settled by his side.

'Isn't it heaven here, on a night like this?'

'That depends on the humans.'

'How d'you mean?'

'It's people who decide whether anywhere's heaven or hell. There are a lot of stupid, selfish, pompous people on this island, but there are also a few nice ones. So I suppose the place is part heaven, part hell.'

'It's funny to hear you . . .' She stopped.

'Funny to hear me talking this way? Why?'

'I'm sure you're being serious and until now you've been so careful never to be serious over anything.' She was silent for a moment, then she continued: 'When I saw you come down here I followed because I've been wanting to say something to you for days, but you seem to do your best to make certain I never have the chance.'

'I've done nothing.'

'You should have been more subtle if you expect me to believe that . . . What's the matter? Have I got the plague?'

'Not as far as I know.'

'That's a relief. But you'd still rather keep me at arm's length?'

'Are you offering an alternative?'

'I'm speaking metaphorically and you know very well I am . . . Alan, I've been trying to apologize.'

He turned and looked directly at her. The moonlight softened her features and added a suggestion of vulnerability. She could be easily hurt, he thought.

She picked up a small stone and threw it. They heard it crash through a bush. 'I want to apologize for reacting so stupidly when you assumed Steve was bedding me.'

'I'd have thought it was I who ought to apologize for making the assumption in the first place.'

'You didn't have much option. I mean, it's not the first time you've come back to find a woman living here, is it?'

'No. But the moment I met you I should have had the intelligence to realize that you came from a different mould.'

'That . . . that's the first really nice thing you've said to

me . . . Years ago, when I was about to go into the great
big world, I promised myself that it didn't matter what
happened, I'd always be honest with myself. So being angry
at you was really being angry at myself because you'd forced
me to realize I wasn't being self-honest any longer. Can you
understand that?'

'I think so. But there's no need to explain . . . '

She interrupted him. 'I had a hell of a year, eighteen
months ago.' She raised her knees and clasped her hands
together in front of them. 'My fiancé decided other grass
was greener and my mother (my father died several years
ago) had a bad stroke and had to go into a nursing home.
She lived for another very long six months, hating the cruelty
of being alive. She'd spent all her married life in a flat—
they once had the chance to buy it, but Father wouldn't; he
lived for the day and forget tomorrow—and she left very
little. I'm not complaining, just trying to paint the picture.

'When it was all over I felt completely empty and I
chucked up my job and came out to Menorca, determined
to try to live as Father had and not to worry about the
future. It was spring and there was the sun and the sea
and people enjoying life and gradually I thawed out. By
midsummer the money was running out and it was time to
return, but I desperately didn't want to. That's when I
heard there was a job suddenly going as a courier. The
woman who'd been doing it was very ill and had to return
to England for specialized treatment and she wasn't expected to return. I'd learned Spanish at school and had kept
it up afterwards, so I went for the job and got it. It finished
in autumn, for the winter, but by then I'd saved enough to
see me through to this spring. In April, I was getting ready
to start work again and make the money to see me through
another year when suddenly the other woman returned,
having made a miraculous recovery. She wanted her job
back. The travel firm were a bit hesitant about getting rid
of me, but I'd known from the beginning the job officially

was only temporary, so I felt I had to bow out grace-
fully . . .

'It's easy enough to make a decision that's morally right,
but it can be hell to have to live with it. Financially, I was
in a tight corner. I tried everywhere for another job, but
when there was a vacancy the employers were demanding
a work permit because the authorities had tightened up and
with all the unemployment in Spain the authorities weren't
really issuing any. It looked like grey skies and a miserable
office job once more when, two days before booking a flight
back, I met Steve in a café in Mahón. We got talking and
he said he was on his own and wouldn't it be fun to have
lunch together? . . . That night we went dancing at El
Molino—somewhere I'd never been near before because it's
so expensive. And afterwards he didn't try anything, but
just dropped me at my flat and left.

'The next day there was another lunch and he asked
me about myself and listened to all my troubles and was
so sympathetic that it made it seem as if things weren't
so hopeless after all. And that's when he asked me why
I didn't come and stay with him here for a while and see
whether I could find a job in Mallorca, where there were
so many more jobs going . . . And before I could refuse,
he made a point of explaining that the offer was only
made because he'd known hard times in the past, so now
that his life was so much easier he liked the chance to
help other people . . .

'Of course, if I'd been honest with myself as I'd always
sworn to be, I'd have recognized the proposition for what it
was. When a man in his late forties tells a woman in her
twenties that he'd like her to stay in his bachelor home
because of the goodness of his heart, she's got to be dumb
to believe him. I was dumb because I desperately didn't
want to return home. And so I persuaded myself that he
was the exception to the rule . . .'

'So what happens now?'

'I don't know what happens now.'

'Still not being honest with yourself?'

'That . . . that's not a very nice thing to say.'

'Why not?'

'You can't see why not? My God! you men can never understand because it's all so much easier for you.'

'What do you really want—sympathy?'

She came to her feet. 'In some ways, your brother's the nicer man.' She left.

He stared out at the moonlit countryside. If he'd given her sympathy, a bond would have begun to be forged between them. And since that could get them nowhere, it could only lead to further heartbreaks for her.

CHAPTER 6

Margaret picked up her appointments diary from the bedside table and opened it. 'We're having drinks at lunch-time with the Piersons and dinner with the Roscoes.'

'I know,' replied Palmer, in the tones of someone who never forgot appointments. He left his bedside and crossed to the nearer window, which was open with the curtains drawn and shutters fast. He pulled back the curtains, unclipped the shutters, and pushed them back against their catches. The air was crystal clear and fresh, scented with pine and wild herbs, but he was more interested in making certain the gardener was working.

The gardener wasn't in sight. Probably he was mucking around with the vegetables in the side bed. Like all the locals, the man was half simple and would insist on growing vegetables on the pretext that one could eat them and one couldn't eat flowers.

'And Amelia rang up to ask if we'd go there at lunchtime Friday week, when her husband is back. I said we'd love to. That is right, isn't it?'

He turned. She was excitingly beautiful, even though newly awakened and tousle-headed. She was wearing a transparent nightdress and her neat breasts were hazily visible. They reminded a man that he was not as old as his passport said.

She replaced the appointments book on the table. 'You do like Amelia, don't you?'

'She's quite pleasant.'

'She has to put up with so much, but she's never anything but cheerful. And she doesn't spend her time criticizing everyone, like some of the dried-up old bitches do.'

He frowned. 'I've asked you before not to refer to people we know in that fashion.'

'How else can I describe them?'

'That is not a very intelligent thing to say.'

All right, so she wasn't very intelligent. But she knew a dried-up old bitch when she met one.

He walked away from the window, stopped when opposite the full-length mirror. Sixty-one and his stomach as flat as a board. Or nearly . . .

'Are you satisfied you'll make Mr Universe?'

If he hadn't known that sometimes she chose the wrong words so that she didn't mean what she said, he might have suspected her of trying to be sarcastic. He gave his stomach a last pat of satisfaction and returned to his bed.

'He's not at all well off, is he?'

'Who?' He watched her breasts and began to contemplate some ding-a-ling, but being a cautious man he remembered their last session had been only two nights ago and at his age—not that he was old—too much ding regretfully often meant not enough ling.

'Pat, of course. Pat Hart.'

'What about him?'

'I said, he's not very well off, is he? I wonder why? I mean, he's clever.'

'Clever?' He considered the possibility. 'No, he's certainly not that.'

'But the other day when he was talking about something to do with astrology, I couldn't understand a word.'

'Astronomy,' he corrected, annoyed by so elementary a mistake. He forbore to point out that whether or not she understood someone was a poor basis for judging that person's level of intelligence.

'Why d'you say he's not clever?'

'He messed up his career.'

'I've never heard that before. What happened?'

'He was with a big firm and doing well and they offered him promotion, but he was sufficiently ill-advised to turn it down. That marked him as unambitious and unable to accept greater responsibility, so when they had to shed part of their workforce due to the recession, they made him redundant.'

'I'd have said he'd lots of ambition and wasn't the least bit frightened of responsibility. Are you sure that's right?'

'He told me himself that promotion would have meant travelling abroad frequently and he wasn't willing to leave Amelia so much on her own.'

'That was the reason? Then it was wonderful of him to turn it down.'

'When he was ruining his career?'

'He was doing it for her.'

'He should have been capable of making a sounder judgement.'

'Are you saying . . .' She stopped. She could argue all day and he still wouldn't understand. She spoke as casually as she could. 'D'you think his cousin will be at the cocktail-party on Thursday?'

'I sincerely hope not.'

'Why d'you say that? I don't think Steve's nearly as bad as people make out.'

'Then you are in a very small minority.'

'All right, he chucks his money around rather, but who wouldn't?'

'Anyone who is not so unmistakably noveau riche.'

'But he was so badly off before . . .'

'It's a matter of breeding.'

'He's very kind to Amelia and Pat.'

'Really?'

'Yes, really. He's let them have that finca for months and months; and a car.'

'He thinks it makes him look good in the sight of others.'

'My God, you've got a nasty, suspicious mind!' She immediately regretted her words. But there had been no need to worry.

'There's a saying in the City—"Probity will earn you respect, suspicion will earn you money." ' He spoke with satisfaction.

'You really can't imagine he might just want to help them? Just because he's inherited a fortune he's beyond the pale, whereas if he'd swindled it out of other people in that wonderful City of yours he'd be a hero?'

'Please don't show how ignorant you are on such matters . . . Why are you so concerned about him?'

She realized that she'd become indiscreet. She forced herself to relax and shrugged her shoulders. 'No reason except I think it's rotten the way some people are always going for him.'

'Manners makyth man.' He looked at the bedside digital clock. 'It's past breakfast time and I haven't heard Ana yet.'

'I expect one of her kids is ill again: they don't seem a very healthy lot.'

'We pay her to start work at nine.'

'But you know what the Mallorquins are like where time's concerned—it just doesn't mean anything to them. Bill says it's because they're one of the few people in the world who've learned that life's for enjoying, not enduring.'

'That's the kind of ridiculous rubbish he would say. And

since you've mentioned his name, I'd rather you weren't nearly so friendly with him. He's a homosexual.'

'Bill's gay? For God's sake!'

'He's not married.'

'Maybe he's got more sense ... Bill's no more a queer than you.'

'I'd prefer you not to couple our names together.'

'That's a great way of putting things!'

It took him several seconds to understand what she'd been getting at. He frowned. 'That is in very poor taste ... Why are you so certain he's not a homosexual?'

'Because a woman can judge a whole lot better than a man. And not because he's been after me in the broom cupboard.'

'Are you quite certain?' he demanded loudly.

She spoke in her 'little girl' voice. 'You can't really think I'd let Bill do anything when I've got my wonderful, wonderful Ray?'

He nodded. It was, he now acknowledged, an absurd thought. Apart from anything else, she was so greatly in his debt. When he'd first met her, she'd been nothing but a brassy receptionist. Phyllis, never realizing the strange twists of fate which lay in the future, had once casually referred to her as 'that little tart at the desk'. Phyllis had died suddenly and after a decent period of mourning he'd married Margaret. He'd taught her to be far less obvious in dress and behaviour and so had changed her from brassy to beautiful. It always gave him a feeling of satisfaction when he saw the covetous way in which other men looked at her.

Downstairs, a door banged. 'There's Ana,' she said.

He checked the time again. 'When you pay her at the end of the week, deduct twenty-three sixtieths of two hundred and fifty pesetas. D'you know how much that is?'

'Four thousand and sixty?'

'Approximately ninety-six,' he said severely.

She wouldn't deduct anything. Ana had a husband who

was not very strong, and five children, and life was a constant battle. She could still vividly remember when for her also life had been a battle . . .

His mind had moved on. 'Make certain you look nice for the Roscoes tonight.'

'All right.' The Roscoes were an elderly and spiteful couple whose continued existence had convinced her that euthanasia was a good thing.

'And don't wear the blue dress again; the one with that extreme décolletage.'

She loved that dress and by any modern standard it was not low cut. But to put the matter in the terms that he would have used, he'd paid the bill and no one was going to get a free ride. Still, she'd dozens of other dresses to choose from. He was many things, but he wasn't mean. Her clothes filled three large cupboards. Sometimes she wondered how much they'd all cost and then she remembered Jean, crying bitterly when her only reasonably smart frock had been torn and she couldn't afford to have it invisibly mended . . .

He left his bed and returned to the window. He stared at distant Llueso Bay. 'I think it's time we gave a party.'

'But we had one last week.'

'That was cocktails.'

There was a knock on the door.

He went over to a chair, picked up a dressing-gown and put this on, carefully tied the cord. 'Come in,' he said in English. He'd made not the slightest effort to learn Spanish. It was not a gentleman's language.

Ana, looking tired and harassed, carrying a tray, entered and wished them good morning. Only Margaret responded. She crossed to one of the small tables and put the tray down, picked up a second table and set that between the beds. She moved the tray to the second table.

'You were twenty-three minutes late,' he said. 'Why weren't you here at nine sharp?'

She looked inquiringly at Margaret. Her English was

poor and when the sénor addressed her he spoke quickly
and loudly, to add to her confusion.

Margaret, who was careless about tenses, genders, and
cases, and who didn't care if she said something amusingly
incorrect, asked in her approximate Spanish if one of Ana's
family was ill?

Ana explained that during the night her husband had had
another of his turns and the smallest one had had a bad
attack of the croup . . . And, because of all her troubles,
would it be all right if she left early to go back to help her
mother look after her husband and her smallest one?

Margaret, certain that her husband would have no idea
what it was she was agreeing to, said that would be quite
all right. Ana left.

He withdrew a piece of toast from the toast-rack and
prodded it with a knife. 'The damned woman simply has
no idea how to make toast.'

'The trouble is, out here they don't know toast as we
know it.'

'They don't know anything as we know it. Far too primitive.'

'Who's primitive—us or them?'

'What an extraordinary question!'

'I was only joking.'

'I do wish you'd understand and remember that there are
some things one simply does not joke about. And that
reminds me, when we're at the Roscoes' don't bring up the
subject of birth control as you did at the Traynors'. The
Roscoes will not enjoy that kind of discussion.'

'From the look of them, they wouldn't know what it was
all about.'

'I . . . I really can't understand you this morning.'

'I'm sorry. A bit of a headache.' She returned to her 'little
girl voice'. 'You aren't angry with me, are you? Margaret
can't live when Ray is angry with her.'

'As long as you remember.'

'Be nice to Margaret, because she's so unhappy when Ray's nasty to her.'

He buttered the piece of toast and added marmalade.

'Does Ray love his little Maggie?'

He nodded.

'A mountainful?'

He did not think it wise to encourage her to that extent. He bit off a mouthful of toast.

She resumed her normal voice. 'Would you like to be a real sweetie to someone?'

'Who?'

'I've been thinking . . . It's just that Steven knows so few people and he's lonely and it would be really kind of you to have him to our party.'

'Steven who?'

'Steve Cullom.'

He'd been about to take another bite of toast. He stared at her across the slice; a glob of marmalade slithered down the side and fell on to his dressing-gown.

'He is so lonely . . .'

'Haven't I made it abundantly clear that I have no intention of entertaining so vulgar a man in my house?'

'But . . .'

'That is quite enough.'

'You're being so stuffy. What if he does chuck his money around a bit? You know why people don't like him, don't you? They're jealous because he's so rich; it's nothing to do with his manners.'

'We will drop the subject,' he said coldly. Then, unaware of any contradiction with what he'd just said, he added: 'Why do you keep talking about him? Why should you be in the least concerned about whether he is or isn't lonely?'

She saw that his mouth had set in mean lines. In a very short time he could get really nasty. 'For heaven's sake, I do believe you're jealous!' She giggled.

'Don't be ridiculous.'

'You think Steve and me have been romping around in the hay. All right, I confess. He's a demon lover and he turns my limbs to water. One look from his piercing eyes and I can't stop him wreaking his every passion on my quivering body . . .'

'You're being very absurd.' But the lines around his mouth had relaxed. He finally took a mouthful of toast. He chewed a couple of times, then said through his mouthful: 'This toast is like concrete.'

CHAPTER 7

Alan Cullom walked out of the house and crossed the pool patio to the glass-topped bamboo table which had been set for breakfast. He sat and relaxed and enjoyed the warmth of the sun . . .

María arrived with a tray which she put down on the table. 'My baker finished his holiday yesterday so I was able to get some ensaimadas for you.'

'The best on the island. As soft and sweet as a virgin's kiss.'

She chuckled. 'And what would you know about them?' Like most Mallorquins, she had an earthy sense of humour. She lifted the plate of ensaimadas, butter, apricot jam, coffee-pot, cup and saucer, sugar, and milk, off the tray and set them out. Then she waited.

He tore off a piece of ensaimada, buttered it, added apricot jam, and ate. 'Absolute perfection.'

She beamed with satisfaction, as if it had been she who'd made the featherlight confection. 'And d'you know what I'm preparing for lunch?'

'Tell me.'

'Pollo ajillo.'

'I can't wait for lunch!'

'And I'm putting in a special lot of garlic for you.'

'Don't tell Steve that.'

'He really likes it, even though he doesn't know he does.'

After she returned into the house, he resumed eating. Susan had talked about a moonlit night being heaven. For him, heaven was eating ensaimadas on a sunny morning by a swimming pool.

Steven Cullom came out on to the patio and across to the table. 'You're good at making yourself at home.'

Alan Cullom noted the tone of anger and knew that there was going to be row; for the moment, he'd no idea why. 'I've always thought of your place as home—rightly or wrongly.'

'Wrongly, when you start abusing the hospitality.'

'All right. What's the matter?'

'What did you do last night after you'd said you were going to bed?'

He finally realized the cause of his brother's anger. 'I decided I wasn't tired enough to turn in and I came down, persuaded Karl into his kennel, and went for a stroll. Susan couldn't sleep either and she found me and we had a chat. I suppose you saw us?'

'That's right. I saw you trying to muck around with my woman.'

'Steve, cool your imagination. We didn't even get around to holding hands.'

'You're a goddamn liar.'

'And you're all fired up because you're up against someone who isn't ready to flop on her back just for a taste of your money.'

'If you—' began Steven, his voice thick with anger, then he cut short the words.

'Surely by now you've understood what kind of a woman she is?'

'I'll behave as I like in my own goddamn house.'

'For God's sake . . . Don't you understand that she'd

never play anyone false and she'd see mucking around with me as playing you false?'

'And just how can you be so certain of that?'

'By knowing her.'

'All this, from one chat in the dark?'

'From seeing her over several days. And from having the wit to recognize someone special when I meet her.'

'You're a bloody liar. And you can leave here. Is that clear?'

'You could hardly have made it clearer.'

'And if you think you're going to get anything out of me, you're bloody mistaken.' Steven stood abruptly, kicked the chair out of the way, and crossed the patio towards the sitting-room door.

María, who'd come out a little earlier, wished him good morning and began to ask him what he'd like for breakfast. He ignored her and continued into the house, slamming the French window behind him and the glass, not being held by putty, rattled so heavily it seemed for a second as if it must shatter.

María, her expression troubled, went up to Alan Cullom. 'What is wrong with the señor?'

'You could say, he's suffering from frustration.'

'I don't understand.'

She waited, but when he said nothing more she shook her head. 'It's very sad when a family has an argument.'

'I shouldn't worry. He'll get over his present problems, one way or another.'

She returned into the house.

He finished the last ensaimada and poured himself a second cup of coffee. Ever since he could remember, Steven had been afraid of being made to look a fool. It was strange, now that he was so wealthy, that obviously this fear had remained with him. Wealth usually insulated a man from everything but the envy of others. But perhaps it couldn't quite abolish the farcical humour inherent in being discovered outside a woman's bedroom, being refused admission ... How had Steve been thick enough to misread Susan's character so completely? True, he'd done the same initially when he'd assumed she was sleeping with Steve, but almost immediately he'd realized his mistake ... Life was endlessly complicated, unless you had nothing. Then your worries were reduced to the problem of where you were going to lay your head after you'd been thrown out of house and home.

The Piersons owned a large house in a new urbanización near the port. When it had been sold to them by the builder, it had been claimed that it had a view of the sea. This was true, provided one stood on the roof.

Amelia Hart moved around the open patio in her wheelchair and wherever she went there was laughter. She had a sharp mind and a lively wit and often took advantage of the fact that because of her infirmity she could say things which, if said by others, might cause some offence. But she was never malicious and her humour was of the ironic, not the banana-skin variety. Frequently, the point of her stories was against herself.

She came up to where Palmer stood and said: 'Ray, you don't know Maurice, do you?'

Palmer looked briefly at the tall, thin man. 'No, we haven't met.'

'Maurice is my cousin.'

'Another?'

'I know, it does become a bit much. And if poor old Basil hadn't been killed in a car crash last year it would have become overwhelming,' said Maurice Ackroyd. 'But since, basically, it's our grandparents who should be blamed, I always plead diminished responsibility.'

'Humph!' said Palmer, who couldn't decide whether Ackroyd was trying to be humorous or was making even more fatuous conversation than was normal at cocktail-parties.

'Pat had to go back home, so he asked me to come out again to be with Amelia. Being of a highly altruistic nature, I came.'

She chuckled. 'Altruistic, my foot! What brought you back was the local wine. I'm the excuse, not the cause . . . There's Maureen. I must have a word with her. She said she'd give me an easy recipe for turron and as the gardener's just given me half a sackful of almonds I want to try and make some.'

They watched her wheel herself across to speak to a large well-dressed woman who was standing by the elaborately built well-head, complete with pulley, chain, and bucket, which was bogus since underneath was a cistern and water was drawn from that by an electric pump.

Palmer, feeling obligated to carry on a conversation, said: 'How long have you been here?'

'Since Monday. I tried to wangle more than a week, but we're short-staffed in the office at the moment so it was no go.'

'What work do you do?'

'Local government: housing.'

Palmer was uninterested in local government.

'I take it you live here?' asked Ackroyd.

'Yes.'

'You're very lucky.'

It wasn't luck which had brought him, it was business acumen and success. But perhaps it was not surprising that a local government official couldn't appreciate that. Palmer looked at his Piaget watch. 'I'd better leave as soon as I've found my wife.'

'You've lost her?'

Palmer said coldly, and pompously: 'One does not lose one's wife in that sense.'

'I don't know about that,' replied Ackroyd cheerfully. 'Quite a lot of men seem to these days. Women's lib demands an equal right to desert. I've always maintained that in such circumstances the only sensible thing to do is emulate Little Bo-Peep.'

'Bo-Peep?'

'Leave them alone and hope they'll come home, leaving their tales behind them.'

Palmer's expression changed from bewilderment to dislike.

Ackroyd, who was nearly four inches taller than Palmer, said: 'Tell me what she's wearing and I'll look and see if I can see her.'

'Thank you, but I am quite capable of finding my wife on my own.' He nodded a curt goodbye and moved away. He had reached the well when his host, a bottle of champagne in one hand, said: 'Where's your glass, Ray?'

'I've had enough, thank you, and we must be off. I have some papers to deal with. Have you seen Margaret?'

'Yes, she was with . . .' He stopped.

'With whom?'

'Bill and Carol, I think it was,' he said, with sudden vagueness. 'Come on, have another drink and leave the papers, along with everything else, for mañana. Those glasses on the tray are all clean.'

Palmer hesitated, then picked up one of the glasses and held it out to be filled. As Pierson moved away, Lionel and Sylvia Bovis came up to him. Sylvia, a striking, well-formed woman, who made-up and dressed in uninhibited style, hugged him. 'I've been looking for you, my grand amour, all evening. Where've you been hiding?'

He never knew how to respond to her ridiculous manner. 'I haven't been hiding anywhere,' he said testily.

'I believe you've been betraying me with some young lady.'

'Don't be so absurd.'

She struck him lightly on the chest. 'There you are—as good as admitting it.'

'I'm admitting nothing.'

'Bloody sensible,' said Bovis, slurring the second word. 'Half the trouble in the world comes from admitting.'

She turned. 'And the other half from drinking anything to hand.' She turned back. 'Ray, my love, I want you both to have dinner with us. Are you free on Saturday week?'

'I think so.'

'Good. And I'll ask the Tippets. You are on speaking terms with them at the moment, aren't you?'

'Of course I am.'

'It's just that one never knows. She can be such a bitch.'

'I think she's a sweetie,' said her husband.

'There's no need to tell us that. You can't keep your eyes off her.'

'It's not my eyes you need to worry about.'

'I don't worry. And in any case, it's no good getting grown-up ideas where she's concerned. Diana likes her men red and raw. It's the primitive in her . . . Ray, where's Maggie. I want a word with her.'

'I am not certain where Margaret is right now,' he replied.

Bovis leaned forward and spoke in a low, confidential voice. 'You ought to keep a closer watch.'

'Shut up!' said Sylvia.

'Don't forget . . .' He swayed slightly and had to shuffle his feet to keep his balance. 'Confucius, he say, old man with young wife need four eyes . . .'

'Lionel's tight again,' she said loudly and unnecessarily.

'So? In vino veritas.' He concentrated his gaze on something beyond his wife and Palmer.

They turned. They saw Margaret, closely followed by Steven Cullom, stepping out of the house. Her face was flushed and his expression was one of anger.

'Very, very veritas.'

'My God, you're a bloody fool,' said Sylvia.

'Probably. But not blind as well.'

CHAPTER 0

Alvarez turned off the road and drove through the open gateway, up over the brow of the hill, and down to Ca'n Cullom. He parked by the front door and climbed out of the car as a man in working clothes came round the far side of the garage. He introduced himself.

'You're not local?'

'I'm from Llueso. Been called out because it's a foreigner.' He spoke with resignation. He'd been cast in the role of troubleshooter in any case which concerned a foreigner, even though Superior Chief Salas seldom hesitated to criticize his methods and results. 'Who are you?'

'Reinaldo Artich, the gardener.'

'You're the bloke who found him, then. Where is he?'

'In the garden, of course. D'you think, seeing as I'm the gardener, I'd be finding him in his bed?'

Alvarez studied the short, wizened man, his face leathered by countless summers of blazing sun. 'All right, suppose you show me where he is. You're quite certain he's dead?'

'Ever seen a bloke with half his head caved in get up and talk?'

They walked past the garage and round the house, then along the path which crossed the lawn to the terraced slopes. Alvarez said: 'My God, there's some work here!' He stared down at the trees, shrubs, and plants which provided a riot of colour and many of which he'd never seen before.'

'And you can't eat one of 'em,' said Artich scornfully. 'The foreigners are bloody fools when it comes to money. D'you see those palms there?'

'Yeah?'

'They were put in with a crane. Each one of 'em cost a hundred thousand. A hundred thousand pesetas, each one!

How many cuaterades could you plant with melons and tomatoes for a hundred thousand?'

Anyone who could spend such a fortune on each of those six-metre-high palms, thought Alverez, had lost all sense of reality. Foreigners were fools. But there folly was dangerous. The young Mallorquins were becoming tainted by such stupidity. They demanded cars, newer and bigger, instead of being content with mopeds—forgetting that twenty years before they wouldn't even have been able to afford one of them . . .

'D'you have 'em in Llueso?' asked Artich.

'Do we have what?'

'Foreigners, of course.'

'Many more than you have in this part of the island.'

Artich shook his head, hawked, and spat.

'Where's the body?'

'Down on the right. The best way to get to it is to climb down—if you try to get along the terrace you've got to push past bushes with spikes long enough to spear your liver.'

They walked along the edge of the lawn, and the first drystone retaining wall, for ten metres, then Artich came to a stop. He pointed. The body of a man lay sprawled out between a rubber tree and a datura with orange-red trumpet flowers.

'Slipped and fell,' said Artich. 'Boozed.'

The head had presumably struck one of the stones of the next retaining wall. He'd fallen in a surprisingly wide arc . . .

'D'you reckon you're up to climbing down?' asked Artich doubtfully, as he studied Alvarez's slack, in parts pudgy, frame.

All his life, Alvarez had suffered from altophobia and even this three metres depth was enough to dry his mouth. But he wasn't going to confess his weakness to a man who'd laugh about it in the bars of Santa Victoria. He knelt, took hold of the largest rock, and very carefully began to lower himself over the edge. Immediately, he became certain he was going to fall and he scrabbled desperately with his shoes for a toe-hold.

'D'you need a hand, then?' asked Artich, highly amused.

Alvarez found one toe-hold, then another. With a courage which only he could evaluate, he released his right hand and took a fresh grip half a metre down, jamming his fingers between two rocks . . .

When he reached the bottom he was breathless, sweating profusely, and his arms and legs were shaking. Sourly, he watched Artich descend without trouble and apparently without effort.

He walked past the datura and stared down. The dead man's expression seemed to be more one of puzzlement than fright or agony. His eyes were half open and they were reflecting the sharp sunshine. The wound was not as extensive as Artich had suggested, nevertheless it seemed safe to assume that the man had not lived for any appreciable time after he'd suffered it. There had been considerable bleeding and the soil about the head was stained; in addition, two of the top rocks of the next retaining wall were bloodstained and on one of them was also some matter that had probably come from the interior of the head.

The ground was dry and hard except where the blood had soaked into it and at one point here something had pushed into it and lifted out a little of the soil; whatever that something was, it hadn't left an identifiable impression, but it was reasonable to assume it had been a shoe. There were no traces of anything lying around or caught up on the nearby bushes and trees.

Alvarez turned and faced the retaining wall he'd climbed down. If someone were standing on the edge there and he fell, it seemed probable that when he landed he would do so well short of where the body now lay. So he could only land sufficiently far out to strike his head on the next retaining wall if he had jumped outwards, at the run, and then had turned half a somersault. Who, knowing the edge was there and unguarded, would have been running?

'The doctor's going to have to get down here, likewise a photographer and two or three chaps to lift him. So it would be best to get a ladder fixed up. D'you have one?'

'We've one up in the shed.' Artich grinned. 'Will you climb up and get it?'

Alvarez maintained a dignified silence.

Ten minutes later, after Artich had lowered a large Mallorquin triangular ladder, Alvarez climbed up to the lawn. He led the way to the shade of a fig tree and produced a pack of cigarettes. The air was so still that as they smoked the smoke rose and only very slowly began to waver.

'They told me on the phone he owned this place,' said Alvarez. 'So I take it he was rich?'

'More money than sense.'

'Was he married?'

'Wasn't no need for that, was there?'

'What's that mean?'

'Couldn't count all the women if I tried. There's one of 'em up there now.' He jerked his head in the direction of the house. 'I'll say this for her, though: she's not the right bitch some of 'em have been.'

'Is anyone else staying here at the moment?'

'His brother.'

'What's he like?'

'A lot younger. He comes and goes and never stays for long.'

'How do they get on together?'

'Not so bad, considering one had money and the other hasn't.'

'There was trouble over money?'

'He was always on about it, thinking he was being done. Went for me, more'n once.'

'Maybe with reason?'

'He couldn't prove nothing—and it's no good you saying otherwise.'

'I'm sure it isn't . . . Have you heard them rowing about money?'

'I've heard 'em rowing a couple of times, but what they was on about I wouldn't know. But María's told me they've been on about money.'

'I take it she works in the house?'

'That's right.' He scratched the back of his neck.

'D'you know who inherits this place?'

'All I can tell you is, it won't be me.'

'What good would it be to you—you wouldn't know what to do with it.'

'Wouldn't I? I'd tell you just what I'd do with it. I'd pull out all them hundred thousand peseta palms and all the stupid plants and bushes, I'd plough up this lawn, and I'd grow things.'

Alvarez stubbed out the cigarette on the sole of his shoe, automatically taking care because of the risk of fire. 'I'd best go inside and talk to 'em. You'll be around when the doctor turns up, won't you, to give a hand?'

'I ain't goin' anywhere.'

Alvarez turned to leave. Artich said: 'Does it matter about the dog?'

'What's the problem?'

'The dog's missing. It wasn't around when I got here and María says it's not in the kennels and she hasn't seen it. I'm wondering if it could maybe have got loose and it'll cause trouble. There's a lot of sheep in the area and I don't know what it's like with them.'

Alvarez asked him about the dog. There'd been a burglary when the señor had lost quite a lot and because of that he'd had the whole estate ringed with a chain-link fence and had bought a guard dog in England . . . Two hundred thousand pesetas. When a man with any sense could buy a dog for five hundred in the market! . . . Last thing every night the dog was released and left to guard the grounds. In the morning, either Artich or María put it back in the kennels. And although it was all right with someone it knew, towards anyone else it could be really savage . . .

'Have you asked the farmers round about to find out if they've seen it?'

'That ain't my job.'

'It is now.'

Grumbling, Artich followed Alvarez up to the house. As they reached there, a Renault 11 drove up and the police doctor brusquely introduced himself to Alvarez.

CHAPTER 9

'It's . . . it's such a terrible shock,' said Susan.

Alan Cullom watched two men through the sitting-room windows; they crossed the lawn and, in turn, disappeared from sight as they climbed down to the first terrace.

'It's only last night . . .' She stopped.

'That he tried to get into your bedroom again?'

'I . . . Perhaps I ought to have . . .'

'Let him in?' He turned round. 'That's just being bloody silly.'

'But afterwards, he must have gone on drinking. If he hadn't, he probably wouldn't have gone out during the night and fallen over and killed himself.'

'So now you're blaming yourself for his drunkenness?'

'How can you talk like that? He was your brother.'

He walked across to one of the armchairs and slumped down in it. 'In other words, I'm sounding like a prize bastard? But it's just that I don't believe death changes the facts and it's hypocrisy to make out that they do. We were half-brothers, but beyond that we hadn't much in common.

Things were better before his wife died and he came into
all the money. That really changed him. People always do
change when they're rich. They can buy whatever they want
and that gets them to thinking they've suddenly grown tall.
And superior people, like politicians, can't stand being
laughed at.' He suddenly came to his feet and walked across
to the cocktail cabinet. 'What'll you have?'

'I don't want anything, thanks.'

'It'll help ease the tensions.'

'I'd still rather not.'

'Pretend it's midday so that in the eyes of the true blue
Brits it's a legitimate and even exemplary occupation.'

'Must you jeer at everything?'

'Haven't you understood that most times I'm really jeer-
ing at myself? A drifter, living for today, never for tomorrow,
shutting his eyes to the fact that what one does today is
payment for tomorrow.' He opened the top of the cocktail
cabinet and this, through a system of counterweights,
brought up a rack of bottles and half a dozen glasses. 'I've
met me, thirty years on, in bars and doss houses all over
the world.'

'Then why don't you settle down?'

He poured out a gin and tonic and opened the ice-bucket
to find that it was empty; he shrugged his shoulders and
drank. 'If ever I start to ask myself that, I give myself the
answer that I'm the exception, that when the time's right I
will have the power and the will to break away from the life
of the lotus-eater, Circe won't capture me and cap me with
a snout.' He drank. 'I've always known I've been lying to
myself, of course, but I've never recognized that I know
this. Double-think has a much longer history than Orwell.
Ten more years of drifting, maybe five, and I'll have had
it.'

'Then why not stop double-thinking and get out of it?'

He looked at her across the top of his glass. 'Is this a good
moment for confessions?'

She didn't answer.

'Tell the truth and shame the devil? Rather, tell the truth and shame oneself. I started drifting in the name of independence and truth; I was romantic and was certain life wasn't to be found in a nine to five office. Steve told me I was a fool and that life meant a secure job, a neat little surburban house, respectability. Then his wife unexpectedly came into all that money and died and he was rich. He was independent. He could have made his own rules and found out what's truly worthwhile and what isn't. But instead he set his sights on buying himself into so-called society, sucking up to all that's meanest in others. It made me laugh, remembering how he'd pontificated at me. And the easiest way of showing him I was laughing was to continue drifting, certain it embarrassed him every time he had to admit to a brother who sometimes didn't know where he was going to sleep the next night . . . So, you see, although I claim a motive of independence, in fact I'm showing a Pavlovian reaction.'

'I think you're talking nonsense because you're far more shocked than you want to admit.'

He finished his drink and poured himself another. 'Have you always looked at the world through rose-tinted glasses?'

'And if I have?'

'It becomes very painful when you have to take them off.'

'One doesn't have to if one doesn't want to.'

'Not even when Steve hammered on your bedroom door?'

'All that did was make me recognize I'd been lying to myself.'

'So there is one time when you don't wear them—when you look at yourself?'

She said in a small voice: 'I'm sorry, but I don't like talking like this.'

He returned to the chair and sprawled out in it.

There was a silence which she broke. 'Alan . . . I'll move as soon as I can.'

'What d'you mean, move?'

'I can't go on staying here.'

'Why not?'

'Surely you can understand?'

'I can understand one thing. It's time you learned to think a damned sight more about yourself and a damned sight less about other people.' He wished he could teach her to become selfish. Then she'd be better able to survive in a world which seldom favoured those who were emotionally generous.

The doctor was a small man, round-faced, with a neat moustache, dressed in a linen suit. He spoke as if he were already late for his next appointment. 'You'll have the body taken to the mortuary right away?' He opened the door of his car.

'It's been arranged, señor,' said Alvarez.

He climbed in, fixed the seat-belt, started the engine, and accelerated sharply up the rising drive.

Alvarez walked slowly towards the outside door of the utility room. The body, the doctor had said, had cooled by eight and a half degrees, which suggested a figure of less than seven hours since death, but it was necessary to remember that it had been a very warm night and that the moment the sun had risen the day had become hot. Rigor had appeared in the face, jaw, and neck muscles, but had not spread to arms and trunk. In view of these facts, he placed the time of death at between two and four in the morning. This estimate was not to be accepted as any more accurate than was normally the case.

The injury to the skull was considerable and consistent with an instantaneous death, but this could only be confirmed by a post mortem. Within the wound were traces of what could be grease. Both stones on which there were bloodstains were rounded, the one which also bore some cranial matter being the more rounded of the two, yet the wound looked as if it had been caused by something fairly pointed. A further point for the PM to consider . . .

Alvarez reached the door. There'd been no grease on either of the stones. They'd have to be carefully photographed and then be equally carefully removed, packed up, and sent to the forensic laboratory. If the evidence continued to come together to suggest thai this hadn't been the accident it had at first appeared to be, a test would have to be devised to show how far out on the terrace a body would land as the result of a straight, simple fall rather than a jump . . . He opened the door and went inside.

The utility room, which was large and tiled, was equipped with washing-machine and tumble-drier, two chest deep-freezers, together with a large air-conditioning unit from which led two large trunks, presumably to serve the whole house. When you were rich you could even defy nature and stay cool in the summer.

María was in the kitchen and her eyes were red from weeping. It was not, she admitted, that she had liked the señor, but when a man died, particularly when he did so unexpectedly, it did not matter whether one had disliked or liked him, one wept. Perhaps as much for this reminder of one's own mortality as for his death.

'He wasn't a very nice man?' Alvarez asked, as he settled on a stool.

She began to prepare the coffee-maker. 'Rest his soul, but he didn't speak our language and he could be terribly unreasonable sometimes.'

'Reinaldo told me his brother's staying here?'

'Señor Alan? He arrived a few days ago and brought me some material from Cyprus. I'm going to have a dress made from it.'

'He's all right, then?'

'He's . . . Well, he could be a Mallorquin.' She plugged in the electric coffee-maker.

'How did the two brothers get on together?'

'I wouldn't know,' she answered, trying, and failing, to sound convincing.

'It seems as if Steven Cullom liked the women. Did they like him?'

'They liked his money.'

'It was like that, was it?'

'Isn't it mostly? I've had 'em in this kitchen, looking round, deciding what to change when they became the señora.'

'But he never got round to marrying any of 'em?'

'Why buy in the market when you can pick for free?'

'Why indeed! . . . One of his women is staying in the house now, isn't she?'

'No.'

'No? But Reinaldo told me there was a woman here.'

'Reinaldo Artich is a fool, just as his father was a fool before him. Neither of 'em with the wit to know a good woman from a bad one.'

'How d'you do that?'

'What's the use of me trying to explain to you?' she asked contemptuously. 'For you men, there's only one way to judge a woman.' She crossed to the large refrigerator and opened the right-hand door to bring out a bottle of milk.

'Are you saying that the woman who's here wasn't after his money?'

'Of course the señorita wasn't.'

'Yet she is staying here, in his house?'

'In her room, not his.'

'How can you be so certain she never moved?'

'Didn't I hear Señor Alan and him arguing . . .' She stopped.

'Arguing about the señorita?'

'Perhaps. What does it all matter now?'

'I'm just trying to get a picture of the people in the house.'

'Let the dead keep the picture.' She went over to the far cupboard. 'I bought some ensaimadas for their breakfasts,

but because of all the terrible trouble no one's eaten any.
Would you like a couple with the coffee?'

'Thanks.'

'And a coñac?'

'How did you guess?'

'I'm married, aren't I?'

Alvarez introduced himself to Alan Cullom and was in turn
introduced to Susan. Her eyes, he thought, were the deep
blue of the bay on a cloudless day: in them was the warmth
of a ripened cornfield. He said he was very sorry about the
death of Steven Cullom, apologized for having to ask them
some questions, and promised he'd be as brief as possible.
Alan Cullom excused himself and went into the house.
Alvarez and Susan sat, she in the shade of a sun umbrella.

He looked at the distant view. 'It's very beautiful here.'

'Yes,' she murmured.

'But perhaps for both of you at the moment that is not a
kind thing? It can make sadness seem so much more bitter
and difficult to bear.'

She was plainly surprised, even bewildered, that he should
have said such a thing. And because of this she thought
about it and she realized that beauty *was* made for happiness.

María was right, he decided. The señorita was different
from all those other women who had come here. She would
never visit another man's bed unless she truly loved him
. . . 'Señorita, perhaps if we start now, we can soon finish.
When did you last see Señor Steven Cullom?'

'When I said good night before going up to bed.'

'Can you say what time that was?'

'Not really . . .' She heard a door open and turned to
watch Alan Cullom come out of the house. When he reached
the table, she asked: 'Have you any idea what time it was
I went to bed?'

Alan Cullom sat. 'Something like half eleven.'

'And had the señor been drinking?'

She hesitated.

'He'd been drinking heavily,' said Alan Cullom flatly.

'Something had upset him,' she said.

'Do you know what?'

'I don't, but he went to a cocktail-party before lunch and he was obviously very uptight when he got back. That's right, isn't it, Alan?'

Alan Cullom nodded.

'And was it because of this that he was drinking so heavily?'

'We're just saying he came back in a temper and spent the rest of the day with a bottle,' said Alan Cullom. 'We don't know any more than that.'

'Did you go to bed at the same time as the señorita?'

'No.'

'After the señorita left, how did he behave?'

'He became more and more argumentative and so in the end I cleared off.'

'Argumentative over what?'

'Everything.'

'Could you be a little more specific?'

'No. I'd had a bit of a skinful myself and the details aren't all that clear.'

Susan was looking both worried and uneasy. Alvarez remembered that María had reluctantly admitted that the two brothers had had a row over her. 'After you went upstairs, did you hear your brother leave the house?'

'I climbed into bed, watched the room go round a few times, fell asleep. If a bomb had gone off, I probably wouldn't have heard it.'

Alvarez half turned. 'Señorita, did you hear anything?'

She hesitated. 'I don't know . . . I suppose that sounds silly? But I wasn't sleeping as well as usual and I suddenly jerked awake and I was certain I'd heard a telephone ringing. Only when I listened, there was nothing. I suppose really I was imagining it. When one wakes up suddenly like that, it's often difficult to distinguish between dreams and reality, isn't it?'

'Whereabouts is the telephone?'

Alan Cullom answered. 'There's one in the hall and one in Steve's bedroom.'

'Could the señorita from her bedroom have heard the telephone in the señor's bedroom?'

'Yes; in fact, much more clearly than the one in the hall. The dividing walls in this place are far from sound-proof.'

'Did you hear talking, señorita?'

'No, nothing.'

'Do you know what time this happened?'

'I've no idea . . . It's really rather silly of me to have mentioned it.'

'Indeed not . . . Señor, did your brother own this house?'

'Yes.'

'And do you often stay here?'

'Whenever I get washed up on the beach.'

'For heaven's sake, Alan . . .' she began sharply.

'Look, Sue, I'm what I am and the Inspector'll find that out quickly enough.'

'And what are you, señor?'

'A drifter. A boat bum. Give it a name, I'll accept it.'

'Sometimes you make me absolutely furious!' She turned to Alvarez. 'Alan's got the awful English habit of running himself down as a kind of inverse boasting.'

'That's a novel interpretation,' said Alan Cullom.

'Is it? What's the difference between you and the million-aire who points to his original Degas and says it's not a bad little painting, is it? . . . Inspector, Alan's been doing something which most people at one time or another have longed to do, but never had the courage. He's seen the world as it really is, not as it appears on TV.'

'I must remember that line of exculpation,' said Alan Cullom ironically.

She turned back. 'And now you're embarrassed to hear the truth.'

'Or uneasy at being painted in false colours?'

'If you won't recognize the true colours, they're all false.'

Under that calm exterior, she was a real fighter, Alvarez thought admiringly. 'Señor, do you know if your brother made a will?'

'I presume he did. He was always careful over that sort of thing.'

'Can you say which solicitor acted for him when he bought this house?'

'I can't. I was thousands of miles away at the time.'

Alvarez thought for a moment. 'Thank you very much for your help. I am sorry to have had to trouble you.' He stood.

Alan Cullom accompanied him into the house and, as they entered the hall, said: 'Can you tell me what happens now? With respect to moving the body and arranging the funeral?'

'Arrangements are being made, señor, for the body of your brother to be taken to the mortuary as soon as possible. There will have to be a post mortem. After that, unless the terms of the will are to the contrary, you will need to speak to one of the undertakers in Santa Victoria to ask him to arrange the funeral.'

Alvarez waited for a moment, but nothing more was said. He opened the front door and went out.

He had just driven through the gateway on to the road when he saw Artich trudging along with the heavy-footed but enduring gait of a true peasant. He turned off the engine and waited. 'Any trace of the dog?'

'No one's seen it. And there's no sheep been savaged.'

'How did it get out?'

Artich shrugged his shoulders.

'Have you ever known it get loose before?'

'Never. It couldn't, not with the fence right round.'

'Did the señor ever put it away in the kennels in the morning?'

'On a Sunday, he must have done because María and me didn't come. Any other day he was too busy to worry about a dog. Only interested in the bitches,' he added, and laughed at his laboured witticism.

Alvarez used the back of his hand to wipe the sweat from his forehead. 'Someone had better tell the guardía rural. It could lead to trouble.'

'Hasn't eaten anyone yet. Unless it had the two strangers for supper.'

'What two strangers?'

'Old Jorge saw 'em yesterday.'

'When?'

'How would I know when?'

Alvarez started the engine again and drove off.

CHAPTER 10

Dolores looked across the dining table. 'Is something the matter, Enrique?' It became clear that he hadn't heard her. 'Enrique, is something wrong?'

He jerked his attention back to the immediate present. 'What d'you mean?'

'You've not said a word.'

'It's just that I've been thinking.'

'About women?' asked Jaime.

'Your mind,' snapped Dolores, 'needs washing.' But she didn't miss the fact that for a second Alvarez had obviously been disconcerted.

'How can Daddy's mind be washed?' Isabel asked curiously.

'It can't, because there's no soap strong enough.'

'Why does it need strong soap?'

'Be quiet.'

Normally, Isabel and Juan, being Mallorquin children and therefore spoiled and often precocious, ignored any orders that were given, but experience had taught them that when their mother's voice assumed a certain timbre it was necessary to do exactly as she said. Isabel asked no more questions but she did wonder whether a detergent would do the job.

'I suppose you've spent the morning on the beach,' said Jaime, envisaging an army of bare-bosomed maidens.

'I've been at Santa Victoria,' replied Alvarez.

Jaime drained his glass. He thought about refilling it, but realized that Dolores was watching him.

Alvarez finished his last mouthful of Frito Mallorquín and asked if he might have some more, it was so delicious. Dolores served him and then, in a moment of absent-mindedness, put a spoonful on her own plate, completely forgetting that she had promised herself to go on a diet. As she ate, she wondered if Enrique had once again been fool enough to become involved with some totally unsuitable woman? Why couldn't he have the sense to settle for a respectable widow who had a nice, clean house and some land?

After his siesta, Alvarez drove to the guardía post. In his room, he settled behind the desk and stared gloomily at all the paperwork on it. His eyelids were becoming heavy when the telephone rang, jerking him wide awake.

'Inspector Alvarez? The superior chief wishes to speak to you,' said the woman with a plum in her mouth.

He waited.

'Alvarez, where is your report?'

'Which one, señor?'

'On the death of the Englishman at Santa Victoria.'

'I haven't made it out.'

'Why not?'

'The initial investigations aren't yet completed.'

'Alvarez, I trust you are not once again, with a faculty which I can only describe as one of perverted genius, about to turn a simple case into a complicated morass of inconsistencies?'

Alvarez felt rather hurt. Why would he be blamed for events which had always been beyond his control?

'Are you still there?'

'Yes, señor.'

'Then would you please be kind enough to answer me.'

It hadn't really seemed to be a question, more a statement of despair. 'At the moment, señor, there are one or two points concerning the death of Señor Steven Cullom which in my opinion need to be investigated further.'

'Perhaps it would be advisable at this stage to determine two facts which in the past have led to endless trouble. Are you certain that he is dead?'

'There's no room for doubt.'

'When a case is in your hands, there is always room for doubt. Is the dead man Steven Cullom?'

'Quite definitely.'

'I am surprised at the progress you have made . . . Now, what are the points which still need to be investigated?'

'On the face of things, the cause of death was an accidental fall down a terrace. But the body landed further out than seems reasonable. And the police doctor says there are traces in the wound in the head which look like grease and that the shape of the wound does not appear to be consistent with the shape of the rocks which are supposed to have caused it. In addition to that, the dog is missing.'

'The dog is missing . . . I confess I fail to see the relevance. Perhaps I have missed something?'

'At night the gates were shut and a guard dog was let loose in the grounds to protect the house; there appears to be no way in which the dog could get out. Yet the dog was missing this morning when the maid and the gardener arrived.'

'Have any of the neighbours seen it?'

'No. But in checking I've discovered that two strangers were in the neighbourhood yesterday.'

'Foreigners?'

'I can't say.'

'Has it occurred to you that it might be important to know?'

'Yes, señor, but so far there hasn't been time to check.'

'Was the dead man wealthy?'

'From the looks of things, very.'

'Who inherits the estate?'

'I haven't been able to discover yet.'

'Are there any women mixed up in the case?'

'He frequently had women to stay.'

'Was one there last night?'

'Yes. But she's different.'

'In what way?'

How did one explain to a superior chief who was a self-satisfied Madrileño that there were in this world just a few women with eyes of warmth and hearts of love . . .

'Well?'

'Señor, from something the maid overheard, it seems reasonable to suppose that the señorita refused to sleep with him.'

'Then why did he have her in the house?'

'I cannot answer that.'

'It might help you in your investigations, Inspector, if you could learn to have a less naïve appreciation of events . . . Report to me the moment you can be certain whether or not this was an accident.'

The connection was cut without even an abrupt goodbye. Alvarez slumped back in the chair. Why was he always expected to have the answers before the questions had arisen? Especially when there were as many questions as fleas on a hedgehog . . . What was Susan's relationship with Alan Cullom? How serious had been the row between the two brothers which María had overheard? Had there been another and more bitter one after Susan had gone to bed? How big was the estate and who inherited it? Was Alan Cullom the man Susan obviously thought him, or had he managed to pull the wool over her eyes because she always believed the best of people? . . .

Worn out, he closed his eyes.

Alvarez had just decided it was time to think of returning home when the telephone rang.

'This is Doctor Verdura. I've spoken to Professor Fortunato, at the Institute of Forensic Anatomy in Palma, and he tells me he hopes to carry out the post mortem next Monday. In the meantime, I have carried out a further, but still necessarily superficial, examination of the dead man. Apart from the wound on his head, there are several areas of bruising on his left side. There are no signs of cellular reaction in these which may indicate that the bruising occurred after death. I can confirm that the shape of the wound is apparently inconsistent with the shape of the rocks which bore the bloodstains. The stains in the wound are almost certainly those of some form of grease.'

'Are you saying that he definitely wasn't killed by falling head first on to the rocks?'

'I am making certain observations that are based on a superficial examination: these observations may be confirmed, they may be denied, by the PM.'

'But he couldn't have picked up any grease from either of the rocks.'

'Can you be quite certain of that?'

'I didn't examine them all that closely . . .'

'Then I suggest that any conclusion be withheld.'

'You wouldn't like to give a . . .'

'I am not prepared to say anything more at this stage.'

Alvarez thanked the doctor for ringing. As he replaced the receiver, he sighed. It looked more and more like murder. Murders created so much extra work for him.

CHAPTER 11

The sargento, a broad-shouldered, pot-bellied man, perpetually bad-tempered because he suffered from chronic indigestion, looked up from his desk. 'Well?'

'Inspector Alvarez, Cuerpo General de Policía, from Llueso.'

'Then you're the bastard who's had all my men wasting their time, tramping the countryside?'

Alvarez gestured apologetically. 'I'm sorry, but I must try and find out where the dog's got to.'

'So my men, with much more important things to be done, have to waste the morning asking every half-witted peasant whether he's seen a stray—' he stopped, searched amongst some papers, found what he wanted '—a stray Giant Schnauzer, eating either people or sheep.'

'Has anyone seen it?'

'No one within three kilometres of Ca'n Cullom has seen anything of it.'

Alvarez scratched his chin. 'Wouldn't you have expected someone to have?'

'With thousands of dogs everywhere?'

'But in this case . . . Anyway, thanks for all your help.'

'Do me a favour, will you? Next time, ask the municipal police. They've nothing better to do.'

Alvarez walked along the arched passageway to the front of the guardia post and his parked car. He sat, began to tap on the wheel with his fingers. To a townsperson, it probably had seemed a ridiculous task. One stray dog. But from dawn to dusk the country people were out tilling their land and harvesting their crops and they saw and noted everything that happened around them—they would have noticed a large, black, wavy-coated dog with docked tail. So the fact that one had not been seen suggested this was possibly because it hadn't been there to be seen. Yet it was missing ... Look at the problem from a different angle. Someone wanted to get into the grounds, but there was the guard dog. So obviously it had to be got out of the way somehow if one were to gain entrance unscathed ...

He left Santa Victoria and drove along the winding lanes, past fields of almond trees, now showing their immature crop, and, where there was irrigation, tomatoes, peppers, aubergines, beans, potatoes, artichokes, and strawberries, to Ca'n Cullom.

Artich was in the small garden room, beyond the garage. He did not hear Alvarez approach and was sufficiently startled to drop his cigarette. 'What are you doing, creeping around the place?' he demanded angrily.

'Relax. I'm not paying your wages.'

He bent down and picked up the cigarette. 'Maybe you ain't. The question is, who is?'

'I can't answer.'

'I'm not working for nothing.'

'Seems to me you're not working.'

'Bloody funny!'

Alvarez sat down on a battered wooden chair. 'Would you like to do me a favour?'

'No.'

'I want you to help me look for a grave.'

Artich's lined face showed a growing uneasiness. 'Who else has died?'

'The dog, maybe.'

Artich drew on the cigarette, exhaled. 'Then the señor's death wasn't no accident?'

'That's what I'm trying to find out.'

He dropped the cigarette on to the concrete floor and stamped it out.

'We'll start up by the gates,' said Alvarez. 'And what we're looking for is newly disturbed earth. It'll have had the sun on it for some time, so it may be a bit difficult to distinguish . . . '

'Not if you use your eyes.'

They walked up the inclined drive to the line of oleander bushes and past them to the gateway. Alvarez turned and studied the land. The garden, in the strict sense of the word, didn't start until the other side of the oleanders, but here the rough grass had been kept cut. Dotted around were trees —he identified mimosa, acacia, jacaranda, and Judas—and over in the far corner, beyond a well, was a thicket of large bamboo.

They began their search and soon Alvarez was sweating so freely that he had to keep mopping his forehead and face. He reached the bamboo. The base of the thicket on the outskirts, where there was plenty of light, was a tangle of brambles, weeds, and grass. He walked down the outside. Three-quarters of the way along, where the bamboos grew less thickly together, he could see perhaps a third of the way through. A square of yellow caught his attention. He hesitated, then stepped inside, easing his way between a couple of very tall and thick bamboos. His right hand caught on a bramble trail and instinctively he flinched to his left; the side shoot of a bamboo which had at some time been broken off dug into his shoulder.

Scratched, breathless, and sweating more than ever, he reached the yellow plastic shopping-bag. Inside it was a small, colourless plastic bag which bore rusty-red traces on the inside and a strip, torn off a till roll, which recorded the purchase of one item at a cost of ninety-five pesetas; below the total were the words, 'Thank you for your custom. Toni, Calle Pescador.' He thought that the stains in the clear plastic bag were possibly those of sobrasada.

A little further in from where he now stood the bamboo grew more thinly and it was clear that the ground tangle of bramble, weeds, and grass, had recently been disturbed. He hung the yellow bag on a bamboo side shoot, continued

towards the disturbed area. Because of the patchwork of
sunshine and shadow, he was very close to the dog before
he realized it was there. It lay, as it had been thrown down,
on its side.

A quick search of the area, difficult and painful, uncovered
nothing of significance. He returned for the yellow bag and
then pushed his way through to the outside of the thicket.
He cupped his hands round his mouth and shouted. Artich
stumped his way over. 'I've found the dog—in there.'

Artich looked at the bamboo.

'It'll be one hell of a job to get it out. I don't know if
between us we can manage . . .'

'I reckon if you give a hand we bloody won't. Whereabouts
is it?'

When Artich came out of the bamboo he was carrying
the heavy body of the dog by its four legs. He dropped it
down on the ground. 'Cut its throat.'

'What's that?'

'I said, its throat's been cut. Can't you see what's in front
of your eyes?'

It was far from obvious as the dog lay, but the moment
Alvarez moved the head he saw the wound. 'Why the hell
do that? . . . Or was . . . There'll have to be a post mortem
to find out exactly what killed it.'

Artich stared at him. 'I've met some stupid buggers in
my time, but if you don't know that cutting a dog's throat
kills it . . .' He hawked and spat.

'Can you find a large sack to put it in?'

Artich, with one last look of contempt, left. He returned
five minutes later with a fifty-kilo plastic bag which had
contained artificial fertilizer. They tipped the dog into this.
'D'you know if Señor Alan Cullom's in the house?' Alvarez
asked.

'He ain't. Went out earlier with the señorita.' He laughed
salaciously. 'She's lost one of 'em, but she's keeping herself
busy with t'other.'

'Hold your filthy tongue.'

'A detective from Llueso! And you don't bloody know what kills a dog or makes a woman happy!'

Alvarez rang the front doorbell and María opened the door. He stepped inside. 'I've found the dog. I'm afraid it's dead.'

'That's not surprising, seeing as it didn't know about traffic.'

'It wasn't killed by a car. It was among the bamboos, up beyond the old well.'

'What was it doing there?'

'Someone killed it and then tried to hide the body.'

She looked bewildered.

'Can we have a bit of a chat?'

'You'd best come into the kitchen. And I suppose you'll want a coñac?'

'I'll not say no.'

'Never met a man who would.' They entered the kitchen and she crossed to one of the cupboards and brought out of it a bottle. She half filled a glass, replaced the bottle, got ice out of the refrigerator and tipped three large cubes into the brandy before passing him the glass.

He drank, put the glass down on the table. 'D'you remember the last time we talked? You told me the two señors had had an argument?'

She did not answer and her expression became stubborn.

'Tell me a bit more about that argument.'

'What business of yours is it?'

'The dog was killed. That means that probably the señor was as well.'

She stared at him with growing horror. 'Sweet Mary!'

'Could you understand the brothers when they were arguing?'

'When people talk English quickly, I don't really know what they're saying.'

'But you probably have an idea of what it's all about, even if you don't understand every word?'

She did not deny that.

'So what d'you think they were arguing about?'

She picked up a cloth and began to dry a saucepan that had already drip-dried on the draining-board. 'The señor was always having women to stay here. Women without the shame to care that when I went upstairs I had only one bed to make. Then Señorita Susan came and I had two beds to make. The señor was angry because he could not understand a woman with pride and self-respect who was not for sale; he was like a child who's refused a new toy and loses his temper. Señor Alan knew very soon what kind of a woman the señorita is. And he told the señor to leave her alone and not to try to force his way into her bedroom. And the señor was furious.'

'They fought?'

'Fought?' Her tone became sarcastic. 'Since when does a man like the señor fight if he knows he cannot win?'

'So what happened?'

'How should I know what happened?'

He finished the brandy. 'On Thursday, Señor Steven Cullom went to a party in the morning. How was he when he returned?'

She looked curiously at him. 'How would you expect? The same as before.'

He said patiently: 'What I really meant was, what kind of a mood was he in?'

'Terrible.'

'Was this to do with the señorita?'

'How can I say?'

'Had she gone to the party?'

'No.'

'Do you know where it was?'

'In Llueso or Puerto Llueso.'

'Whose house was it at?'

'I can't say.' Then she added, 'But perhaps it's written down.'

They went through to the hall and she showed him the appointments calendar on the small telephone table. There was an entry for Thursday which read: 12.30. Piersons.

He opened the drawer of the table and brought out the telephone directory. Under Llueso, there was no Pierson listed. He turned to Puerto Llueso. Pierson, Ca'n Blanch, s/n, Calle Juan Villemont.

He looked at his watch. If he left now, he would be at Llueso just before lunch-time. A visit to the Piersons would have to wait.

CHAPTER 12

The Piersons had been in the diplomatic service (his wife had, naturally, assumed his rank) and so although life in retirement had, force majeure, taught them some facts of life, it had not yet persuaded them to speak, especially to a native, without a touch of righteous condescension.

'I'm sorry, but we have no idea,' said Pierson, a tall, lean man, with clipped speech and moustache, and definite opinions on everything, especially those subjects about which he knew little or nothing.

Alvarez, who had not been asked to sit, said: 'You did not see or hear anything which would account for Señor Steven Cullom being so upset?'

'I believe I have already said not.'

'Who did he talk to?'

'You really cannot expect me to be able to answer that. As the host, I was exceedingly busy.'

'Surely, señor, you noticed him talking to someone?'

'You should realize something,' said Clara, a woman who prided herself on always speaking her mind. 'We're sorry to learn that Steven Cullom has suffered a fatal accident, but that does not alter the fact that he was not one of our friends.'

'Certainly not,' confirmed her husband, as he brushed his moustache with crooked forefinger.

'Yet you invited him to your party?'

Pierson was amused by the naïve suggestion that one asked only one's friends to a cocktail-party. His wife said coldly: 'His cousin wanted us to invite him because he knows so few people on the island.'

'One could hardly mention to her,' murmured Pierson, 'that however many people he wished to know, few would wish to know him.'

'Why was that?'

'The fellow was—how can I explain it to a foreigner?— unable to appreciate that a surfeit of money can never compensate for a lack of background.'

'Was his cousin at your party?'

'Yes,' Clara answered.

'Can you tell me where she lives?'

'Not offhand, no.'

'Would you be very kind and look up her address?'

Somewhat piqued, she stood and left the room, unaware that with buttocks the shape and size of hers, a pair of tight-fitting slacks were far from flattering. When she returned, she said: 'Ca'n Oñar,' and sat.

'I think I know that name. Who is the señora?'

'If by that you mean what is her name, it's Mrs Hart.'

'And does she live in a wheelchair?'

'She doesn't "live" in a wheelchair, but she does make use of one whenever she wishes to be mobile,' replied Pierson.

Alvarez thanked them for their help and left. When he was out of earshot, Pierson remarked to his wife that it was no wonder crime in Spain was increasing at such a rate since the police didn't wear ties.

Alvarez drove along the main Palma road, circling Llueso,

and then turned off to the left. When he reached Ca'n Oñar, Amelia was handforking fertilizer into some large clay pots, set a metre up from the ground. He began to introduce himself, but she broke in to say that she remembered him from February. He said how sorry he was that her cousin had died.

She stared out across the garden to a field of orange trees. 'He was so very kind, letting us stay here, lending us the car . . . But I'm not a hypocrite so I'm not going to say that I'm really cut-up. We were cousins, but we really didn't have much in common and although I always tried to be friendly, because basically he was so lonely, there were times when I'd have loved to tell him to pull himself together. And then there were the family stresses and strains.'

'I beg your pardon?'

'It's what my mother always said when I was young and she didn't want me to understand what was going on. But I'm sure you don't want to be bored by family history.'

'On the contrary, señora, I would like to hear it.'

She frowned. 'Why?'

'Because I think I will have to investigate the death of Señor Cullom more closely and it will help to know all I can about him.'

'Oh! . . . Are you really saying it may not have been an ordinary accident?'

'I'm afraid it probably wasn't.'

'That is a bit of a shaker.' She put down the handfork. 'I thought of having a cup of tea earlier on, but with Maurice down in the port I just couldn't be bothered. As you're here now, would you like some?'

'Very much, señora.'

'Good. Where would you like to be? Out here or inside?'

'Outside, unless it is too hot for you.'

'It's never too hot for me, especially when I remember that we're going to have to return to the sad English climate . . . So sit down while I get it.'

He sat and imagined himself the owner of this finca and he thought how full his heart would be as he ran his fingers through the rich soil . . .

She returned, a tray balanced on the arms of the wheelchair. 'Will you be mother?'

He was startled.

'You obviously don't have the expression out here! It means, will you pour out the tea.'

He lifted the tray from the wheelchair and set it on the table.

'No milk for me, thanks. I have it with a slice of lemon and try to forget how much nicer it would be if I dared to have sugar and milk. But I can't stand saccharine in tea and sugar's so quick to put on the pounds.'

He handed her the filled cup in which there'd been a slice of lemon. 'You want to know about the family Cullom,' she said. 'It's an odd family, but perhaps no odder than others. Grandfather Cullom had four children and for some reason I've never been able to fathom they disliked each other. To such a ridiculous extent that every time one of their children did well at something, there was a fearful crowing . . . Inevitably, the pointless antagonisms were passed on. People can be incredibly silly.

'Anyway, Mark Cullom married twice and had Steven by the first marriage and, much later on, Alan by the second. Steven didn't do well at school, got a poor job, and married Agnes—at the point of a shotgun, the rest of the family claimed—a no doubt worthy but exceedingly dull woman. After his marriage there were scandals concerning other women, at least one of which threatened to become serious. My mother and Aunt Prudence, the only surviving parents by then, were delighted by all this and when Alan turned out to be a wanderer who wouldn't, or couldn't, settle down to a respectable life, their cup was overflowing.' She chuckled. 'Unfortunately, their cup turned out to be cracked.

'When Agnes's mother had died, she'd left Agnes a little money and some shares, presumed to be almost worthless. Out of the blue, the shares turned out to be worth a fortune.

'Agnes's sudden wealth changed her completely. From being meek and mild and ready to put up with most things, she became quite aggressive and she told Steven that if he didn't stop chasing other women she'd make certain he didn't enjoy another penny of her money. That brought him to heel. Then, quite unexpectedly, she became seriously ill and died within a month. In her will, she left everything to Steven. Both my mother and Aunt Pru died within a year of her. I've always thought that their resentment at seeing their black sheep of a nephew inherit so much was at least partially responsible for their deaths.

'As regards us cousins and how I thought of Steve . . . If I'm honest, I have to say that I was envious of him, in the way that one normally is envious of people who are so much better off.' For a moment she paused and it was not difficult to judge that she was thinking of all those who were better off than she, not in financial terms but in physical ones. 'But the traditional family dislikes hadn't rubbed off on me, nor was I bitter because he was the black sheep and his iniquities had been rewarded . . . So you can see, I'm sad he's dead, but not shocked as one is when someone close and dear dies. I don't know whether you can understand what I'm trying to say?'

'Indeed, señora.'

She looked at him. 'I've always thought detectives must become very hard people, not allowing themselves to appreciate emotions, because they have to deal with so much sadness and brutality and becoming hard is the only way in which they can protect themselves, but you haven't, have you? Do you get hurt often?'

He didn't answer.

'Yes, you do. And I should never have asked so impertinent a question. My mother once told me I ought regularly to wash my mouth out with vinegar, but I never understood why vinegar should stop me asking questions.' She finished her tea. 'Has any of that helped you at all?'

'I think now I know a little more about what kind of a man the señor was.'

'Earlier on, you said that you might have to investigate Steve's death more closely because it wasn't an ordinary accident. That must mean you think someone may have killed him?'

'Yes.'

'Why should anyone have done that?'

'I don't know yet.'

'Then you came here to try and find a motive?'

'Señora, I am sure you cannot possibly answer that question directly, but everything you tell me builds a little of the picture and therefore you may be able to help me indirectly.'

'What a bloody world it can be!'

He waited a moment, then said: 'Did you see much of him?'

'In England, before he moved out here, no, not very much. Apart from anything else, we lived over a hundred miles apart. But since he first lent us this place, which he bought before his present one, we've naturally seen quite a lot more of him. As I said earlier, basically he was a very lonely man. He needn't have been. Out here, most people are prepared to be friendly and they'll cross social boundaries which they'd run away from at home. But Steve saw boundaries which weren't there and he thought he could breach them by flaunting his money. The result, of course, was to build them.' She moved the wheelchair three or four metres to her right, then returned; as someone not crippled might begin to pace, gaining a measure of satisfaction or relief from the movement. 'I think he came here to see me. Pat was always friendly, of course, but he did feel that anyone with that much money who behaved as Steve did was stupid, and that sort of attitude usually shows, however much one tries to hide it. I didn't see things like that. I think people behave as they do because that's how they're conditioned. When Pat said Steve was a fool for trying to use his money to buy friendship, Pat was making an objective criticism. But I'm sure Steven really couldn't help acting as he did. And maybe my sympathy showed . . . And there's probably another reason why he came. Being chairbound made me different and he came to think of me as an agony aunt.'

'A what?'

'The women in magazines whom people in trouble write to to ask for advice when they can't face those near to themselves. Not that with Steven it was a case of asking for advice. That would have needed some degree of humility. His need was for contact with someone other than . . .' She stopped.

'Yes, señora?'

'You'll have learned about his visitors?'

'You mean, the ladies?'

'In the circumstances, "ladies" is the wrong word.' She smiled wearily. 'And there's me making an objective criticism? Maybe they were so desperate for friendship, even if falsely given, that if the cost was the use of their bodies, they were prepared to pay.'

'He told you about them?'

'To the extent that sometimes I decided he was boasting and said so. But nothing worried him until . . . He told me about one woman—girl, I suppose. Kept on and on about how sweet and innocent she was and how their relationship was justified because she brought out all that was best in him. I said that if she was as sweet and innocent as that, he was a swine to corrupt her and twice a swine to try to justify himself so hypocritically. That offended him and he left here in one hell of a rage. He did come to see me again, but things weren't the same. I don't think that what annoyed him was the fact that I'd accused him of corrupting her, it was because I'd called him a hypocrite. Rotters so often

seem to be unable to admit to themselves their rottenness.'
Her voice sharpened: it became almost angry. 'But I wasn't
going to take back anything I'd said. He'd behaved like the
out-and-out rotter the rest of the family had always called
him. This girl wasn't a foreigner who was probably as
experienced as he, but was truly an innocent. By seducing
her, he was damning all foreigners on this island.'

'Do you know the girl's name?'

'He must have mentioned it to me, but I can't remember
it now. He always told me their first names and I noticed
something strange—they were always rather exotic.
Samantha, Gwendoline, Henrietta and never a Jane or a
Mary. Do the Samanthas lead giddy lives while the Janes
stay at home and marry, or is it pure coincidence? . . .
Pat says I've a political mind; always concentrating on
inessentials. And because my mind's so birdlike, I've just
this second remembered the girl's name. Beatriz.'

'Beatriz! . . . What was her surname?'

'He never mentioned surnames.'

'Where does she live?'

'He didn't say that either . . . Do you know her?'

'I may do,' he answered bitterly.

'Oh my God!' She moved the chair until she could reach
out and grip his forearm. 'Please. If you find you do know
her and she was terribly upset by what happened . . . Please
don't blame all of us for what one of us did.'

'Of course not,' he answered. But he knew fresh and even
more bitter resentment at what the foreigners had done to
his land and his people.

She released his forearm and wheeled the chair back to
where it had been. 'Is there anything, anything at all, I can
do to help?'

'No.'

They became silent, each deep in thought. He was the
first to speak. 'Señor Steven Cullom was at a party on
Thursday and you were also there?'

'Yes.'

'Did something happen there to upset him?'

'I . . . I don't know.'

It was obvious that for the first time she had been less than honest. 'Señora, this is very important.'

'So am I supposed to indulge in some nasty, vicious gossip?' She sighed. 'Sorry, I'm making a fool of myself. But I can't stop thinking of Beatriz. Is she . . .' She saw the look on his face and immediately understood that he would tell her nothing because it was a shame which had come to a fellow Mallorquin. 'With women, Steven could be incredibly stupid. From something I heard, instead of restricting his affairs to foreigners who were right outside the community here, he'd become over-friendly with the wife of one of the local "pillars of society".'

'And the wife was there on Thursday?'

'Yes.'

'And was the husband also there?'

She nodded.

'Does he know what is happening?'

'I can't answer . . . And I wish to God I hadn't told you because there's probably not a scrap of truth in the beastly suggestion.'

'What is her name?'

'I'm not going to tell you.'

He rubbed his chin. He said sadly: 'Do I have to go back to Señor Pierson and ask him?'

'So that that wife of his gets her bitchy claws into the story and makes a banquet out of it? . . . You're a lot harder than you appear, aren't you? You're willing to use a form of blackmail to make me tell you the name.'

'If it was murder, I have to find the murderer.'

'And to do that you're prepared to risk ruining other people's lives?'

'Sadly, the innocent so often suffer.'

She stared out and watched a large, iridescent dragonfly

dart past. 'Yes, they do.' She again moved her wheelchair until she could touch his arm. 'At some time in your life, you've been innocent yet suffered a great deal, haven't you?' He hesitated, then nodded.

'It's strange, but suffering so often brings out compassion in someone, rather than a sense of resentment. It makes me think that God must have a sense of irony.' She took her hand away. 'Will you be compassionate?'

'I will do what I can.'

'You must promise me one thing. I only heard about it from Sylvia Bovis. She's someone who dramatizes every-thing and perhaps what she says happened doesn't really mean much. Talk to her first. If you find it was like that, there'll be no need to go stirring up trouble, will there?'

'None at all, señora.'

'Thank you,' she said softly.

CHAPTER 13

Lionel Bovis's speech was slightly slurred, his movements were studied, and his gaze was sometimes unfocused. Sylvia was dressed in a black trouser suit with an elaborate pattern in gold-coloured thread and depending on one's taste she looked either exotic or tarty.

'Have a drink?' said Bovis.

'Mary Tudor had Calais engraved on her heart; no prizes for guessing what's engraved on my husband's heart,' said Sylvia. A keen ear could catch contempt as well as resig-nation in her voice.

Alvarez sat. The room was large and furnished expen-sively, with some Spanish pieces and some from either Britain or France. The mixture made for neither smart formality nor cheerful informality.

'Well, what's it to be?' asked Bovis, as he stood in the

middle of the Chinese carpet. He began to sway slightly.

'A small coñac, please, señor.'

'You're asking for something he's not familiar with,' she said. 'He reckons small drinks are what one gives to birds.'

'Dolly birds,' said Bovis.

'In your state, you wouldn't know what to do with a dolly bird if she fluttered straight into your lap.'

'I'd pluck her, of course.' He chuckled as he carefully walked over to an elaborately inlaid cocktail cabinet.

'No one can accuse you of having a demanding sense of humour . . .' She turned and spoke to Alvarez. 'So what can we do for you?'

'Señora, have you heard of the death of Señor Steven Cullom?'

'Haven't heard about anything else.'

'I am making some inquiries.'

'Why?'

There was a cold glitter to her wide, bright eyes and he thought of a snake, ready to coil itself around its prey. 'Because his death may not have been an accident.'

Bovis spoke from across the room. 'What d'you . . . What d'you . . .?'

'We've reached the cracked record stage,' she said. 'You're saying Steve may have been murdered?'

'Yes, señora.'

'Well, well, well! We do see life in this neck of the woods.'

'Why should . . . Why should anyone want to . . . to kill him?' Bovis asked. 'I mean . . . I mean, it's not as if he was married, is it?'

She said to Alvarez: 'Why come here, to us?'

'To find out if you can help me with my inquiries.'

'We hardly knew him.'

'I believe you also went to the party at the Piersons' house on Thursday?'

'We did,' said Bovis loudly. He began to cross the floor, concentrating very intently on the tumbler in his right hand. 'And d'you . . . d'you know what? All he offered was champagne. What's the good of that except to . . . to fill the belly with gas?'

'Why complain?' she asked. 'It was alcoholic.'

Bovis held out the tumbler and Alvarez hastily took it.

'What d'you want to know about the party?' she asked.

'Did Señor Cullom meet a lady there?'

'If he . . . he did, he was bloody lucky,' said Bovis. 'I didn't . . . didn't see one.'

'You weren't in any condition to see anything an inch beyond your nose,' said his wife.

'Who was the lady?' Alvarez asked.

She shook her head. 'Forget it. I know what some people have been saying, but it's none of their goddamn business.'

'It has become my business now, señora.'

'Then the best of Spanish luck to you, but I'm not passing on that sort of talk.'

Alvarez remembered what Amelia had said. Presumably, Sylvia Bovis reckoned it was all right to gossip to her own nationals, but not to the Spanish police.

'It's . . . it's not all talk,' said Bovis. 'Our Maggie's got . . . got hot pants.'

Her expression hardened. 'Shut up, Lionel.'

'You can . . . can always tell. And that pompous . . . pompous old idiot . . .'

'For God's sake, shut up.'

'He . . . he won't be able to do much to cool . . . to cool her down, will he?'

'Who won't, señor?'

Bovis looked surprised. 'Ray, of course.'

'Ray who?'

'Ray Palmer, her husband. Don't you . . . don't you know anything?'

'You bloody fool,' she said bitterly.

He stared at her. 'What have I . . . have I done now?'

She said to Alvarez, 'Steven had a reputation and so every

time he spoke to a woman some people's tongues would start chattering. But it didn't meant a damn thing.'

Bovis spoke loudly. 'Are you . . . are you saying our Maggie wasn't sweet on Steve? Then why . . . then why were they together at that hotel in Palma?'

'You've never mentioned that before. You're lying.'

He tried to put his finger to his lips, but missed and struck his chin. 'Don't . . . don't let on. It's a secret and I promised never to tell.'

The sun was low and would soon dip behind the mountains; shadows were long and they brought relief from the heat. The breeze had died away and the air was almost still, yet a couple of windsurfers were trying to sail. The Parelona ferry, bringing the last of the day-trippers back from that beach, carved a white swath through the cerulean waters of the bay.

Susan, wearing a neat bikini, turned on to her side and studied Alan Cullom, who was lying on his stomach. 'D'you know, you haven't said a word for the last ten minutes.'

'When it's like this, who wants to talk?'

'I do.' She brushed some sand off her side. 'I need to know why you're still keeping me at arm's length?'

'Am I?'

'When I suggested going out for the day and getting away from everything, you weren't exactly enthusiastic.'

He made no comment.

'And all the time we've been here, you've been acting like I'm bad news.'

'Where's it going to get either of us to act any other way?'

'For God's sake, how d'you know how anything's going to get anyone until it happens?' She turned back on to her stomach and rested her head on her right forearm. 'Are you a lot more cut-up about Steven's death than you want anyone to know?'

'Stiff upper lip and all that jazz?'

'Christ, I could hit you where it hurts!'

'Not while I'm lying this way down.'

'Always the side-stepping answer . . . Is something more wrong?'

'Why d'you go on and on asking questions?'

'Because I want some answers.'

'Forget both answers and questions. Remember, this is the island where there's no past and future, there's only now.'

'If you lived by that, you wouldn't be acting as you are.'

'How am I acting?'

'Every time I want to talk about something, you duck, you weave, and you circle.' She sat up. She wrapped her arms around her legs, interlocking her fingers. 'Shall I tell you something?'

'If you want to.'

'When I decided to come to this island and stay with Steve, I was being incredibly naïve. But there was something more to it than just that . . . Have you ever had the feeling that if you do something the whole of your life will be changed?'

'Not since I put a tin-tack on the form-master's chair.'

'Ducking, weaving, and circling once more. Are you so scared of admitting to any emotional weakness? . . . I had that feeling in Menorca. So when I came to Ca'n Cullom and discovered that Steve's sole aim and object was to get me into his bed I realized that it was the same old world as before and I felt as if I'd been terribly cheated. Then one morning I was trying to make better friends with Karl and he suddenly ran off. I shouted to whoever it was to stand still and came up past the oleanders and . . . and it suddenly seemed as if maybe I hadn't been cheated after all.' She turned and looked at him; his eyes were closed. 'Have you been listening?'

'Of course,' he answered vaguely, making it clear that he wasn't really interested in a woman's romantically exaggerated emotions.

She nibbled at her upper lip. She wanted to give because she longed to receive, but he would neither receive nor give. If only she hadn't met Steven at that outside café table in Mahón ...

Dolores managed not to refer to what had happened until the children had left the house to play with friends in the street and Jaime and Alvarez were drinking the first of their 'digestive' brandies. Then, instead of removing the tablecloth, brushing down the table, and going through to the kitchen to wash up, she sat opposite Alvarez. 'Enrique, something is wrong, isn't it?'

'Maybe he thought the caldereta was salty?' suggested Jaime.

'Would you hold your tongue until you've something sensible to say,' she snapped. 'I've never used too much salt in my cooking in the whole of my life.'

'No, of course not,' he said hastily, feebly trying to repair the damage of his facetiousness.

She studied Alvarez, her proud, strong, handsome face expressing sharp concern. 'What is troubling you?'

'Nothing is,' he answered.

'Is there some way I can help?'

'There's nothing to help with.'

'But there is trouble?'

'All that's happened is, I've been thinking.'

'About that woman?'

'No.' He shook his head. 'About another one.'

'Another! Sweet Mary!' she murmured, aghast.

Jaime whistled. 'I'll tell you one thing, if I had your problems I'd look a sight more cheerful than you do.'

'We all know,' she said, glad of the opportunity to be able to vent a little of her uncertain irritation on him, 'that nothing would make you happier than to be with any number of women younger and far more attractive than me.'

'I wasn't meaning anything like that. All I was saying was, if I was Enrique—'

'You'd make an even bigger fool of yourself.'

Jaime drained his glass.

She leaned forward and spoke earnestly. 'Enrique, you must listen to me. You must remember that to know a foreign woman is to be with trouble. And to know not one, but two at the same time . . .' She stopped, unable accurately to express such potential catastrophe.

'What the devil are you talking about?'

'These women. This second woman . . .'

'She's married.'

'You're really living it up,' said Jaime admiringly.

'Married!' exclaimed Dolores in tones of horror.

'Here, you're not thinking . . .?'

'But what else can we think?'

'Then I'm sorry for you. Señora Hart, who's confined to a wheelchair, is happily married. She's one of the warmest people I've ever met and wouldn't muck around with another man, not in a thousand years. And all you can think is . . .' He shook his head.

Dolores did not like to seem to be in the wrong. 'All right. Then what about this other foreign woman?'

'It just so happens that she's half my age.'

'Since when did that have any effect except to make you twice the fool?'

'And she has a man of her own age.'

'Oh! . . . Then if that's all true, why have you been so quiet?'

'Because the caldereta was too salty.'

She stood, moved the bottle of brandy, heaped up the plates and carried them out to the kitchen, furious but ever-dignified.

On Monday morning, the duty cabo at the guardia post in Palma Nova telephoned Alvarez. There was a butcher called

Toni in the Calle Pescador at the back of town. Alvarez thanked him, replaced the receiver, and slumped deeper in the chair. When he had been alive, Steven Cullom had sown unhappiness: now that he was dead, that unhappiness was being reaped.

CHAPTER 14

Beatriz had returned to her work in a shoe shop near the front at Palma Nova and she was searching along the rows of shoe boxes when she saw Alvarez enter. Her face crimsoned.

He came up and kissed her on both cheeks and asked after her family, to the annoyance of the blue-rinsed, heavily made-up, middle-aged Englishwoman who expected instant service.

'And how are you?' he asked Beatriz.

Instinctively, she looked down first at her wrists, where the scars were still noticeable, then at her stomach.

A woman came out of the inner room. Neat, precise, with the tight expression of someone who knew to the last peseta how much should be in the till, she studied him, noting the crumpled safari shirt, creased cotton trousers, and scuffed shoes. 'What do you want?'

'A word or two with Beatriz.'

'You ought to know better than to come here during working hours.'

'Cuerpo General de Policía.'

She looked startled, then defensive. 'I've made no complaints.'

'Quite. But like I said, I want a chat with Beatriz so you'll have to run the shop on your own for a bit.'

'Is anyone going to serve me?' asked the Englishwoman in a loud voice.

Like most Mallorquins, the owner put profit before pride. She hurried over and apologized profusely for the delay in broken English.

Alvarez led the way out of the shop. 'Would you like something to drink?'

Beatriz shook her head.

'Then let's get away from here.'

Once they were in the car, he made a U-turn to head up the sloping road and away from the sea. Even more than most, he hated the stretches of coast which had become concrete jungles because he could remember them as they had been—silent beaches, backed by fields wrapped in a soul-renewing loneliness.

They left the built-up area and continued through the countryside until they reached a lay-by on a small rise, backed by scrub land which was littered with boulders. He switched off the engine and stared through the windscreen at the fields, so beautiful with their crops. Inwardly, he sighed. Always, one searched for beauty; so often one discovered ugliness. Always, one tried to bring happiness to others; so often one brought distress and pain . . . 'Beatriz,' he said, and he turned to look directly at her, 'was his name Steven Cullom?'

Her face seemed to freeze, as a face often did under shock.

'I'm desperately sorry to have to tell you this, but he's dead.'

For a time she was kept in suspension by the shock, then she began to cry.

Feeling clumsily useless, he put his arm around her to try to give some comfort.

'Would you like to go home?'

'They don't know,' she murmured brokenly. 'They mustn't know.'

Forty years before, a Mallorquin woman who had an illegitimate baby would have been shunned: which was not to say that unmarried women never became pregnant. When they did become pregnant the father was almost invariably the woman's novio and he married her. Then, when the tides of the permissive age washed over the island tragically to alter all standards, there were many more premature pregnancies and the father was not always a novio, ready to marry. But because standards had changed, understanding had broadened, so usually such women, together with their illegitimate children, were not banished from their homes. But still there remained one barrier which, among those Mallorquin families who held as far as possible to the past, no woman could breach and still remain of the family. She could not bear the bastard of a foreigner. Throughout history, every conquered people had reserved their most lasting hate for those among themselves who had transgressed the commandment, Thou shalt not love thy enemy . . .

The world never stopped for grief and although Beatriz had learned that lesson once, she was going to have learn it again. But a mother's love could make that learning a little less painful . . . Soon, he'd take her home. From her mother he'd learn where Amadeo worked . . .

Amadeo and Félix walked up to the bar in the small café in one of the side streets of Portals Nous. Félix said: 'What the hell have you got us here for?'

'Félix . . .' began Amadeo urgently.

He ignored his brother. 'The head waiter kicked up hell because I had to leave just as the tables needed setting. What d'you want?'

Experience had taught Alvarez to recognize guilt. He sighed. 'Tell me what you want to drink.'

'I just bloody well want an answer,' snapped Félix.

Amadeo, worried by the effect his brother's belligerence might have, begged him to calm down. Then he said they'd both like a coñac.

Alvarez ordered the drinks from the small, facially scarred man behind the bar. 'Let's sit down.'

'You've still not answered me,' snapped Félix.

Alvarez picked up his glass and walked over to a corner table by one of the windows. After a moment's hesitation they followed him.

'Well?' demanded Félix, as soon as he was seated.

Alvarez said: 'I want to know where the two of you were last Thursday.'

Amadeo's shocked fear was immediate and apparent. Félix tried to hide his by blustering. 'What's it to do with you? We've a right to . . .'

'You can tell me now. Or you can wait until we're down at the nearest guardia post.'

The barman brought over two glasses of brandy, put them down on the table, and left. The two brothers drank quickly.

'Where were you?'

'Where d'you think we were?' asked Félix.

'I don't know. That's why I'm asking.'

'I was at the hotel, of course.'

'All day?'

'The foreigners want their grub, don't they?'

'And you?' Alvarez turned to Amadeo.

'I was at the office.'

'So if I question your bosses, they'll confirm what you've just said?'

They looked at each other, then away as they realized how closely they were being watched.

'An Englishman died on Thursday night,' Alvarez said. 'He lived a few kilometres out from Santa Victoria. D'you read about him in the *Diario de Mallorca*?'

'No,' replied Amadeo hoarsely.

'It was originally reported as an accident. In fact, it's virtually certain he was murdered.'

Amadeo lifted his glass to drink, found it was empty. Alvarez turned, caught the bartender's eye, and held up three fingers. 'You were both near the Englishman's house on Thursday.'

'No,' said Félix violently.

'You went there to find the man who'd seduced your sister.'

'We don't know who it was; she won't tell us his name.'

'Someone told you it was Steven Cullom.'

'I swear we were at work all day . . .' began Amadeo.

'All right. Then when we leave here we go and speak to your bosses.'

It became obvious Félix had realized that, since cunning was needed and not a bull-headed approach, he should remain silent. It was Amadeo who said: 'The truth . . . Look, we know two women and they had a free day and so we told our bosses we were ill. We were with them all the day.'

'Their names and addresses?'

'We . . . we can't tell you that. They're married.'

Alvarez said to Félix: 'Do you remember the last time we met? You swore you'd kill the man who'd seduced your sister.'

Félix struggled to contain his panicky temper. 'I was just talking wild.'

'And on Thursday you acted wild.'

The barman brought the three drinks to the table, picked up the three empty glasses, and left.

'What happened at Ca'n Cullom?' Alvarez asked.

'We've never been near the place,' Amadeo answered.

'Two strangers were seen in the neighbourhood.'

'All right, but it wasn't us.'

'D'you know the Calle Pescador in Palma Nova?'

The abrupt change of subject left them bewildered and uneasy. It was several seconds before Amadeo said: 'Of course we know it. Why?'

'D'you ever buy meat at Toni, the butcher's?'

They looked at each other, hoping one of them could

understand the significance of the question.

'Well. Have either of you?'

'No,' said Félix. Desperately worried as he was, he still spoke scornfully—domestic shopping was a woman's job.

'Then you've not recently bought any sobrasada in Toni's?'

'We've just told you.'

Alvarez finished his drink. 'I want your identity cards.'

'Why?'

'I'm going to have the photographs copied. I'll show the copies to the man who saw two strangers near Ca'n Cullom on Thursday.'

'It wasn't us,' said Amadeo.

'Then I'll be able to sort out one question . . . Let's have them.'

Very reluctantly, they produced their identity cards and passed them over.

'One last thing before we go off and find a copying place. Neither your sister nor your mother knows that you know who Steven Cullom was. Keep it like that.' But for how much longer could they be protected from this further hurt? he wondered.

CHAPTER 15

Léroux's grandfather had been a Frenchman who'd come to live in Mallorca because at that time there had been no extradition treaty between the two countries. Three years later he'd married a Mallorquin widow, somewhat ugly but possessed of good properties. Léroux's father had been a quietly spoken, almost deferential man who, just before the outbreak of the Civil War, had had a charge of embezzlement laid against him. Luckily—and the Léroux were, on the whole, extremely lucky as well as sharp—his accuser

had been of socialistic leanings and so when war broke out
and Mallorca declared for the Right, he had been denounced
—by someone unknown—and had disappeared. Blessed
with such inherited talents, it was small wonder that Léroux
had chosen to become a solicitor.

He was a short, butterball of a man, with a jolly face, a
ready smile, and a pleasantry for every occasion. He was a
dandy in dress and even in midsummer he wore a linen suit.
He owned a number of properties, in various names to avoid
confusing the tax authorities, and he became very indignant
if ever it was suggested that a couple of the most valuable,
once belonging to foreigners, had come to him in any but
the most straightforward ways. 'In my profession,' he often
said, 'there has to be trust, respect, and honesty.' He meant,
of course, on the part of the client.

He waved Alvarez to a seat. 'We've never had the pleasure
of meeting before . . . In what way may I serve you, Inspector?'

'I'm investigating the death of Señor Steven Cullom.'

'A very sad case; a charming man.' He rubbed the palm
of his hand over his jet black hair. 'You say you are "investigating" it—then it was not an accident?'

'Almost certainly not. You handled his affairs, didn't you?'

'I certainly acted for him on occasions.'

'Did he make a Spanish will?'

'Indeed. I naturally advised him of the perils of dying
intestate in Spain.'

'I'd like to see a copy of it.'

Léroux used the intercom to speak to a secretary. Then
he rested his elbows on the desk and joined his fingertips
together. 'Presumably, you believe the contents of the will
may be of some significance?'

'They could be.'

'And have you any idea yet who may have killed him?'

'None at all.'

A young woman, neatly dressed, a ring on her engagement

finger, came into the room, smiled formally at Alvarez, put a blue folder down in front of Léroux, and left.

Léroux opened the file and looked through the papers inside. He brought out two documents. 'I have copies of the Spanish will, dealing with his property in this country, and an English will, dealing with his property there.' He leaned forward and carefully placed the two sets of papers down on the far edge of the desk.

Alvarez read through the Spanish will first. The house, grounds, and contents, were left to his brother. The English will was slightly more complicated and he found some initial difficulty in understanding the legal terms, but the import soon became clear; there were six bequests of five thousand pounds each to named charities and then the remainder of the estate went to his brother. 'Have you any idea how much money he had in England?'

'The equivalent of about a hundred million pesetas.'

'How much?'

'A hundred million,' repeated Léroux, a faraway look in his eyes.

A hundred million pesetas, thought Alvarez. With that, a man could buy untold hectares of rich, irrigated land, and grow incalculable tonnes of wheat, barely, beans, tomatoes, peppers . . . He brought his thoughts back to reality. 'What's his house worth?'

'He paid twenty-two million for it and prices have risen steeply since then—say fifty million. And then there's his other house. I didn't act over that, but from what he's said about it, it must be worth at least another fifteen million.'

'And the whole lot, virtually, goes to the brother?'

'If he didn't actually execute a new will, yes.'

'Was he intending to, then?'

Léroux brought a sheet of paper out of the file and read through his notes. He looked up. 'He came here some little time ago to consult me about making a new will in view of his forthcoming marriage.'

'His marriage?'

'You didn't know about it?'

'No one's mentioned it. Who was she?'

'He never named her.'

'Why not?'

'How should I know?'

'Wasn't that odd?'

'He was a foreigner.'

'Did he say what he wanted a new will to be like?'

Léroux looked back at the sheet of paper. 'Everything on this island was to go to his wife. He added to me that he was also leaving everything in England to his wife, except for some bequests to charity and something to his bother.'

'Did he name an amount?'

'No.'

'But he never executed either second will?'

'I gave him the draft of the Spanish one, but he never brought it back.'

'He might have taken it to someone else to execute?'

'Why should he have done that?' asked Léroux in injured tones.

'A check with Madrid would very quickly make certain?'

'Naturally.'

'And the existing British will—who drew that up?'

'I can't tell you.'

'You've never seen it?'

'Never.'

Alvarez thought.

Léroux spoke softly. 'There are a lot of people who'd commit murder for a hundred and sixty-five million!'

Alvarez looked up and thought that he was probably staring at one of them.

Alvarez drove from Santa Victoria to Ca'n Cullom. María opened the front door and told him that Susan Pride and Alan Cullom had left an hour before and she didn't know how long they'd be away. 'It's good to see them get out and forget all that's happened.'

'You think they'll be able to do that?'

'They're young, aren't they? When you're young, you can forget anything.'

'We couldn't.'

Just for a moment she was sad. When they'd been young there'd been the war and no one had been able to forget the hunger, the bitterness, and in particular the grubby little notes, often almost illegible, which arrived by post and said baldly that Juan or Bartolomé or Francisco had died fighting for God and Spain . . . She spoke robustly. 'But what's it matter how things were when we were young?'

'Perhaps if they realized, they would sometimes think of others and not just of themselves.'

'Would you think of anyone else if you were lucky enough to be like them?'

'Maybe not.'

'Then let 'em be.'

'All right. I need to look round the house.'

She hesitated. 'Hadn't you better wait until they get back?'

'I've not the time.'

'Then if you must, I suppose you must.'

'Where did the señor keep all his papers?'

'Like as not, in the study.'

The study lay beyond the sitting-room. It was quite small and was lightly furnished, obviously without any attempt to impress, and was cheerfully, even attractively informal in character. At one end was a kneehole desk and the two bottom drawers, one on each side, proved to be locked. He unlocked them with an adjustable skeleton key confiscated from an elderly housebreaker. Both drawers contained loose papers and files.

He found a photostat copy of Steven Cullom's Spanish will, signed and registered, and a further copy of his English will. In addition, pinned to the English will with a paperclip, there was a letter from a firm of English solicitors to the effect that the original of the will was in their strong-room. He found neither the draft of a new Spanish will nor of a new English one. Nor was there any reference to the identity of his future wife.

He made a note of the name and address of the English solicitors before replacing all the papers and files in the drawers. He returned to the kitchen.

'Did Señor Steven Cullom ever talk to you much?'

María shook her head. 'It wasn't easy because my English isn't good . . . And in any case, he wasn't the kind of man to be bothered to talk much to the likes of me.'

'So he never mentioned about getting married?'

'I can't see him marrying, not all the time there's more than enough sluts around willing to lie down for him.'

Steven Cullom, he thought, had intended to make his wife his main beneficiary. To this end, he'd had a draft will drawn up. Yet he'd apparently never signed the new will and had it executed, nor even named the bride-to-be. Why not? More irritating, unanswered questions . . . 'I'm going out to have a word with Reinaldo.'

Artich was standing by the cultivated circle of earth around a lime tree on which the fruit had formed but had not yet begun to swell.

'Care for a fag?' asked Alvarez.

They smoked and stared at the scene set out before them. Beyond the terraces, a flock of sheep had been turned into a field whose forage crop of barley and oats had been cut, sun dried, and collected.

'D'you remember saying a couple of strangers had been seen around here last Thursday?' Alvarez finally asked. 'Who told you about 'em?'

'I said, didn't I? Old Jorge.'

'And who's he?'

'Everyone knows that. Old Jorge Buades, lives first

place on the right past the bottom of the hill.'

They became silent once more. A red kite passed overhead. Bees were working a nearby jacaranda in late bloom. In the distance, a man was singing a song of unmistakable Moorish origin.

'I'd best be moving on,' said Alvarez, as he dropped his cigarette stub on the ground and carefully stamped it out.

'Never known a bloke so restless.'

Alvarez walked up the sloping lawn. Restless? Not by inclination. He should have stayed on the land, as his forefathers had.

He reached his car and sat, mopped the sweat from his face and neck before he drove off. Beyond the entrance gates, he turned left and went down the hill. At the first farm Buades, an elderly man with bowed shoulders, was irrigating several rows of bush tomatoes—opening up channels to fill them with water, then closing them with a plug of earth. Alvarez waited, knowing it was not a job which could be interrupted, and it was a quarter of an hour before Buades turned off the stopcock on the estanque.

After Alvarez had introduced himself, Buades rubbed his hands together to remove some of the dirt, then said: 'D'you feel like something?'

They sat in the shade of the patio and drank a harsh red wine, made by Buades the previous season and cooled in the refrigerator. Alvarez took two copy photographs from the breast pocket of his shirt. 'Reinaldo, up at Ca'n Cullom, tells me you saw a couple of strangers around last Thursday?'

'That's right.'

'Would you recognize 'em again?'

'Never saw one of 'em that clearly, but I'd know the other.'

Alvarez passed the photographs across. Buades picked them up, studied them for a long time with screwed-up eyes, then put them down. He drank.

'Well?'

He prodded one with his stubby forefinger. 'He was one of 'em.' The photograph was of Félix. 'Thanks,' Alvarez said heavily, trying and failing to hide his bitter sadness.

He returned to Ca'n Cullom, parked outside the garage, and walked round the house. Artich had moved, but not very far; he was now standing in the shade of a fig tree whose sharply shaped leaves were bright and whose fruit was the size of peas. 'Can you find a thin sack, roughly one metre eighty long?' Alvarez asked.

Artich considered the question. 'I might,' he admitted.

'We'll need to fill it with earth so you might think about where's the best place to get it. And you'll need something to do the filling with.'

Artich left, to return a few minutes later with a plastic sack and a mattock. He then led the way over to the far edge of the lawn where he pointed to a wide bed of earth, dug but not yet planted up. 'You can use some of that.'

'I'll hold the sack, you fill it.'

'Bloody hell!' said Artich disgustedly.

Between them, they filled the sack, a difficult operation with a mattock, but a mattock was traditionally the tool to use and Artich would never have broken with tradition by using a spade.

'Now what?' muttered Artich, who was sweating heavily despite the fact that he was in hard condition.

'We carry it over to the point at which the señor fell.'

They set the sack at the edge of the terrace and, at Alvarez's order, upended it. Alvarez stepped back, leaving Artich to keep it balanced. Steven Cullom had been drinking heavily. He had reached the edge of the terrace, taken a step forward without realizing what was happening, and had fallen; or he had caught his foot and had gone sprawling; or he had jumped. It was impossible to imagine why, when drunk, he should have jumped. So whether he had merely stepped into space or had gone sprawling, his feet must have been close to the stone face as he began to fall. 'All right.

Let go.' As Artich released his grip, Alvarez pushed the top of the sack as hard as possible.

The sack fell in an arc which took its head well away from the retaining wall. Yet the stone edge of the next wall still lay a further two metres out. This was confirmation, rough as it was, of what he had accepted from the beginning.

'That's it, then,' he said. 'You can clear things up.'

'On me own?'

'That's right.'

'Leave the other poor sod to do all the work?'

'I find life's much easier like that,' Alvarez replied.

CHAPTER 16

Alvarez sat at the desk in his office and stared through the opened window at the wall of the house opposite. Until he heard from the pathologist's office he couldn't officially call Steven Cullom's death murder, but from the moment he'd found that the dog had had its throat cut he'd had no doubts.

Murder was often a spur-of-the-moment crime, sometimes a carefully premeditated one. This murder came within the second category. So there had to be a discernible motive. Someone had once said that there were a thousand and one ways of murdering someone, but only two reasons for doing so. Money and sex. That was truer than most generalizations. Both elements were present in this case. Steven Cullom had treated women as disposable items and he'd been too self-satisfied to begin to understand that some women asked a high price—love; he had been worth a hundred and sixty-five million pesetas.

Alvarez searched the drawers of the desk for a telephone directory and eventually found it in the bottom right-hand drawer together with a third-full bottle of Soberano and a glass. He poured himself a strong drink. When he'd finished that, he had another. Finally, he checked in the directory on how to make an international call.

When the connection was made with Halscombe, Peeble, and Wraight, in Stentonbridge, a cheerful, youthful woman asked him whom he wished to speak to? He began to explain that he needed to discuss a matter concerning Señor Steven Cullom . . .

'What's that?' she asked. 'I'm sorry, but I can't understand what you're saying.'

He spoke more slowly and simply.

'Hang on a minute, will you?'

He could just hear her say to someone else that there was some queer old man on the phone with a hilarious accent who wanted to speak to one of the partners about a Steve Cullom. Old? One was said to be as old as one felt. Right now, he felt a hundred and twenty . . .

A man identified himself as Byfield and asked how he could help.

'Señor, my name is Inspector Enrique Alvarez, of the Cuerpo General de Policía, stationed in Llueso, in Mallorca. I am investigating the death of Señor Steven Cullom. Do you know the name?'

'Indeed.'

'Did you also know that he was dead?'

'I had no idea of that, no.'

'It is very probable that he was murdered.'

'Really?' said Byfield in careful, neutral tones.

'I have been through his papers and have found the copy of a will drawn up by your firm. I understand from his Spanish solicitor that his estate in Britain may be worth a hundred million pesetas or five hundred thousand pounds, very roughly. Is that right?'

'Speaking from memory, yes.'

'I also understand that he was intending to marry again and to make a second will in England. Would this second one cancel the first?'

'That can be a little tricky. A second will revokes a first
one if it expressly revokes it or the first one is torn, damaged,
burned, and/or its clear revocation was intended. If there's
no express revocation, the new will will only revoke those
clauses which clearly become inconsistent. Marriage automatically revokes a will unless the existing one specifically
states that it's made in contemplation of a particular marriage.'

'Did you draw up a second will?'

'I believe we did, yes.'

'And did that refer to a coming marriage?'

'I would have to consult it before I could answer you for
certain.'

'Would you be kind enough to do that for me, please?'

'Certainly, but it'll take a little time to check through our
records down in the strong-room. Probably, it would be best
if you ring back.'

'Certainly, señor. And perhaps then you could tell me
some details of the new will? And also whether his future
wife is named.'

'You don't know her name?'

'Not yet.'

'Strange. But then I don't feel I'm being unduly critical
when I say that in some respects he was a strange man . . .
Suppose you get back on to me in an hour's time?'

Alvarez looked at his watch. 'I shall be having lunch
then.'

'You don't have to make do with a sandwich at the office
desk? Lucky fellow! . . . All right, let's make it in two hours.'

That would be siesta time. 'Unfortunately, I have something very important to do then, señor. But if I might phone
you at half past five, our time?'

Alvarez was late back at the office so that it was just after
six when he rang England again.

Byfield said: 'The draft of his second will is quite straight-

forward. It specifically revokes all previous wills and states
that it's made in contemplation of his forthcoming marriage.
It leaves his estate to his wife, subject to five bequests; these
are, four of one thousand pounds each to named charities,
and one of fifty thousand pounds to his brother.'

'What is his wife's name?'

'As far as I can make out, he never gave us her name.
I've been through all our correspondence and quite recently
we wrote to him pointing out that in the past the term 'wife'
has led to legal problems where the testator's marriage has
subsequently been called into question and that it is essential
to name the lady. And, of course, as I mentioned this
morning, if a will made before marriage is not to be revoked
by marriage, it has specifically to state that it's made in
contemplation of a particular marriage; the term 'wife' is
clearly general rather than particular . . . We never had a
reply to this letter. I gather you found no trace of the draft?'

'None whatsoever. If the señor never signed the second
will, is the first one still good?'

'If the second will was not signed and witnessed precisely
as required, it is invalid and the first will still stands.'

Alvarez thanked the other, said goodbye, and rang off. In
one English will Alan Cullom had been left a fortune, in the
other fifty thousand pounds. Fifty thousand, on its own, was
a lot of money, but not when matched against many times as
much . . .

He phoned the Institute of Forensic Anatomy and asked
if Professor Fortunato had completed his post mortem on
Steven Cullom and whether tests had been carried out on
the dog. An assistant said that no, it had not as yet been
completed, but it could be said that the bloodstained stones
could not have inflicted the skull wound. Further, the traces
within the wound were of grease; there was no sign of grease
on either of the stones. The dog had been fed a meat-based
mixture, to which had been added a lethal dose of a derivative of chloral hydrate shortly before its death.

'Did you say a lethal dose?'

'That's right. The derivative's only been developed and produced in the past few years and it's very much stronger than the original. The dog ingested several times the amount that would have rendered it merely unconscious.'

'How long would it have taken to work?'

'Difficult to be precise, but certainly no longer than ten minutes; more likely, something under five.'

'Would it have been obvious that the dog was dead?'

'Unless the person were blind.'

After he'd replaced the receiver, Alvarez began to tap on the desk with his fingers. Until now, he'd assumed the sobrasada had been fed to the dog to dull its alertness, create an air of friendship, and distract its attention long enough for the killer to get close enough to cut its throat. But the dog had been drugged and the killer would have waited until the drug took effect. Then, since it must have been obvious the dog was dead, why cut its throat? Unless it had been a perverse act of retaliation?

The Bovises' home was on the side of the mountain at a point where this had become steep and so, in order to provide a firm platform for its foundations, it had been necessary to build it several metres above the level of the road. Thirty-three steps led up from the road to the front door and by the time he'd climbed the last of these, Alvarez felt as if he'd tackled Puig Mayor. As he tried to regain his breath, slow down his heart, and mop up some of the rivulets of sweat, he stared out at the view which led right across to the mountain-ringed Llueso Bay. No view, not even one as grand as this, was worth such agony.

The front door was opened by Ana. Being cousins, if of the very extended variety, they discussed their families at some length before she led him through the sitting-room, one of the largest he'd seen, to the pool patio beyond at the side of the house.

Palmer, an untidy, pot-bellied figure in bathing trunks, was dozing in a deck-chair. At first, Alvarez took him to be unfortunately deformed, but then he realized that the 'deformity' was a nose-shield. Margaret had been lying face down on a towel and when she heard them approach she raised herself on to her elbows and looked to see who they were. She was not wearing her bikini top.

'It's Inspector Alvarez,' said Ana in Spanish.

Palmer jerked awake. For a second he was too confused to do anything, then he snatched off the nose-shield. 'Margaret, your costume,' he snapped. He turned to Ana. 'I've told you a dozen times, never bring anyone here unannounced.'

'Señor?'

'Can't you understand simple English?'

'Please, more slowly . . .'

'Hopeless!' He waved at her to leave, impatiently watched Margaret secure her bikini top. 'Well,' he said to Alvarez, 'who are you and what do you want?'

Alvarez explained. He heard Margaret draw her breath in sharply. Palmer, in his most pompous tones, said: 'Why bother us in this matter?'

'Because I understand you may be able to help me since you were friends . . .'

'We certainly were not. We barely knew the man.'

'But I have been told . . .' Alvarez suddenly stopped. He'd been looking at Margaret and he had seen the fear in her eyes. Clearly, now was the time to tackle her over her friendship with Steven Cullom—when she would be off-balance and unable to lie convincingly—but equally obviously to do this would be to subject her to a great deal of unpleasantness at the hands of her husband. And the case had already caused so much suffering and unhappiness . . .

'Well?' Palmer demanded loudly.

'I have been told you were friendly with him, señor.'

'Then you have been incorrectly informed.'

'Darling, don't you think . . .' Margaret began, her voice sharp with worry.

He interrupted her, certain she wanted to suggest he were more polite. 'Is that quite clear? We were the most casual, and on our part reluctant, acquaintances only.'

Margaret stood, picked up the towel she'd been lying on, and hurried into the house.

Alvarez said: 'Thank you for your help, señor.'

Palmer nodded.

Alvarez returned to the house. In the hall, he called out: 'Ana.'

A door on his left opened and Ana stepped from the kitchen into the hall.

'Ana, I want to get a message to the señora, but I'd prefer the señor not to know about it. Could you have a word with her on her own?'

'That's easy enough. But if I speak in Spanish, the señor won't understand even if he is around.'

'Then tell her to ring me at the guardia post in three-quarter's of an hour's time; that's at half past six.'

She looked curiously at him and he wondered if, absurd as the thought might be, she imagined he was trying to fix an assignation?

The telephone on Alvarez's desk rang. 'What is it you want?' Margaret asked, her voice high.

'Señora, I would like to speak with you, please,' he answered, with cold formality. 'I think it will be better if your husband does not hear what I have to say. So will you meet me somewhere that is convenient?'

'I . . . I can't help you.'

'I am certain that you can.'

'Oh God!'

'Can you drive to Playa Nueva?'

'Yes, but . . .'

'In the port there is a bar on the front which is called

Bardino. I shall meet you there in half an hour's time.'

'But what am I to say to Ray to explain why I'm going out?'

'Perhaps you can give the same reason you have given in the past, when you have been meeting Señor Steven Cullom.'

He heard her stifled cry and it made him think of a child who suddenly discovered that the world was not made exclusively of sugar, spice, and all things nice.

Playa Nueva consisted of three distinct entities. There was the old town, once ringed with a fortified wall, whose history went back to Roman times; the port, which in turn consisted both of a commercial port serving ocean-going ships and a marina for the ever growing number of yachts; and the modern tourist development which stretched along, and blighted, what had once been one of the finest beaches on the island.

Bar Bardino faced the marina and, since the prices were only twice what they were in the backstreet bars, was popular with yachtsmen. Alvarez settled at one of the tables set out on the pavement, under an awning, and ordered a brandy. It had just been brought to the table when he saw Margaret, walking along the pavement.

He held a chair out for her and she sat. She stared at him, frightened, trying to summon up a resistance and failing.

He offered her something to drink. She chose a coffee.

'Do you smoke?'

She accepted a cigarette and smoked it with nervous urgency.

'Señora, earlier you heard me say to your husband that I am investigating the unfortunate death of Señor Steven Cullom.'

She looked out to sea. Within a few days, she had experienced longing, despair, rejection, resentment, anger, and shock, and now she wasn't quite sure what her emotions were.

'You knew him well, didn't you?'

She shook her head.

'I'm quite certain that you did.'

'I . . . I swear I didn't.'

They watched the passing traffic, the scavenging gulls, the yachts ghosting along in the very light breeze, and the ferry leaving port on its way to Menorca. The waiter brought the coffee.

He spoke quietly. 'I have talked to someone who said more than he meant to. He told me that once he saw you and Señor Steven Cullom together in a hotel in Palma.'

She clenched her right hand until her knuckles whitened.

'Your husband does not know about the señor and the hotel?'

She turned to look directly at him, her expression one of complete despair. 'D'you think I'd still be living in his house if he did? He'd kick me out so quickly I wouldn't have time to pack a bag. Don't you understand, he'd go crazy if he had to believe that someone else was enjoying what he'd paid for?'

She'd spoken with a bitterness he'd seldom heard equalled. She'd suffered, he thought. By definition, a woman who betrayed her husband was a good-for-nothing bitch— but was there not occasionally a wife who would have to be a saint not to betray him? And was anyone a saint before she died, when all temptation was left behind? . . . 'Señora, will you come for a short drive with me?'

'Why?'

'Because I have just learned that I made a stupid mistake when I asked you to meet me here.' He drained his glass.

Between Playa Nueva and Cala Bastón, lying back from the coastline, was a marshy area, very well known to ornithologists for the wide variety of birds to be seen there. There had, of course, been grandiose schemes to drain and develop it, but by some miracle of self-restraint on the part of the authorities this had not yet happened. There were a

number of tracks, especially where there had once been salt
pans, and if one knew the route one could drive almost to
the centre and find a solitude, more rewarding to those who
liked their world to be round and soft rather than sharp and
hard, than that to be found in the mountains.

They sat on weed grass. From beyond a belt of reeds there
came a croaking birdcall, with two notes criss-crossing; an
osprey flew overhead.

'What can you tell me about him?' he asked.

She lay back and closed her eyes. The sunlight, reaching
through reeds, created a patchwork of light and shade on
her face. She looked younger, less knowing, more vulnerable.
'I was introduced to him at a cocktail-party several months
back. I knew what kind of a man he really was. After all,
I'd had enough to do with his kind before I married Ray.

'It's funny how life goes. You swear you'll do something
and nothing will ever change that and you really mean it;
then you meet someone and you forget all your wonderful
resolutions . . . I promised myself I'd never let Ray down.
I owed him that, even if he was the kind of man he is. He'd
given me the chance to break loose from the mess that was
my life and that was the least I could do to repay him . . .
The trouble was, it became so bloody boring. I began to
feel as if I'd been trapped into old age. I tried to make him
understand, but he couldn't . . . or maybe wouldn't. And
there was something else . . . I'm still young enough to be
keen. Know what I mean?'

He nodded.

'He tried hard, but sometimes it wouldn't work and he'd
get furious and blame me. And the next time he'd be in a
state so it wouldn't work again and I'd be blamed even
worse . . . I met Steve and he didn't know what that sort of
trouble was. I went in with my eyes open, all right—the
trouble was, my bloody mind closed up. His kind want kiss
and run, especially with other men's wives; the freedom of
the bed, but no risk. So when I started getting fond of him,

he back-pedalled. That made me try harder to hold on to him, so he back-pedalled even faster and soon he was out of sight . . .'

'What happened at the cocktail-party?'

'I hadn't seen him for ages and I was desperate. I made him go into the house with me. I begged him to fix a date . . . He told me it was all over, like yesterday's news. He was so goddamn callous about it; I hated him for not even trying to wrap it up and make it look nice and give me something to remember . . . Christ, how I hated him then! And yet . . . And yet when I heard he'd died . . .' Tears welled out of her closed eyes and slid down the sides of her cheeks.

'Did your husband realize you'd spoken to him at the party?'

'All he saw was us coming out of the house together.'

'Did that annoy him?'

'He thought about it and decided it didn't,' she answered with sudden, fierce scorn. 'After all, we might have met only a moment before and have been discussing nothing more exciting than the weather. So if he became angry it made it obvious he thought something was going on, and if he thought that he was admitting by inference that I might be two-timing him because he wasn't the great big husband he liked to think himself.'

'Suppose he'd decided that you and the señor had discussed more than the weather—would he have been very annoyed?'

'Are you serious? He'd have gone mad from jealousy and shattered dignity.'

'Mad enough to do something about it?'

'He'd have gone for me, if that's what you mean?'

'And for Señor Steven Cullom?'

'Where would he have found the guts to do anything like that?'

'Might he not have wanted to hurt Señor Steven Cullom as a warning or to get his own back?'

'You're not thinking . . .' She sat up. 'You're not thinking he could have had anything to do with Steve's death?'

'Someone killed him.'

'Ray wouldn't have had the courage even to think about that.'

'It might not need too much courage to think of finding someone to act for him.'

'And leave him with the possibility of the bloke being found out and talking? Not in a thousand years.'

He reached out and picked a stalk of rough grass and began to run his finger and thumb along it. Provided the murdered never talked—and was he likely to?—was there really much of a risk? After all, he'd arranged for the murder to appear to be an accident, so the police would not be looking for a murderer . . .

'He couldn't have done anything like that,' she cried wildly.

That would be the final, crushing blow, he thought. To discover that the man she'd loved had been killed by the husband she despised . . . 'Did you know that Señor Steven Cullom was intending to get married?'

Her expression changed and it became bitterly scornful. 'You can call it a marriage if you like. I'd call it something else.'

'When did you first learn about it?'

'He told me to help make it very clear he'd finished with me. I laughed in his face. It's the only time I managed to get through to hurt him.'

'What is her name?'

'Lady Molton. And d'you know why he was hoping to marry her? Not because there was a song in his heart. Because he reckoned that then people would have to accept him. He never realized they still wouldn't, not in a thousand bloody years.'

Love and hate, two sides of the same coin. 'Have you ever met her?'

'Several times. She's a great friend of the Bigsetts and

they, according to some, sit on the right hand of God.'

'What kind of a woman is she?'

'She lives for horses and if you don't know a fetlock from a forelock, you're dead ignorant and uninteresting.'

'But she's very attractive?'

She laughed wildly. 'Attractive? If she'd a slightly longer nose, you'd mistake her for a Welsh pony.'

'Does she live on the island?'

'No; on Menorca.'

'And she was intending to marry him?'

'How the hell can I know what anyone else intends?' As the barred sunlight rippled across her cheeks, she began to cry again.

CHAPTER 17

Alvarez spoke to Superior Chief Salas over the phone, detailing the course of the case. At the conclusion, Salas said: 'I suppose I should not, by now, be surprised that you've succeeded in confusing the issue to the extent that you have. Nevertheless, I have to confess that I am.'

'Señor, it has not been easy. If you look at things . . .'

'If I look at things, I do so logically. Was Steven Cullom murdered or did he die accidently?'

'It is virtually certain he was murdered.'

'Was he wealthy?'

'He was very wealthy.'

'Who inherits his money?'

'That depends on whether his second wills were executed. I don't think either of them was. In that case, except for half a dozen small legacies, his brother inherits everything.'

'Then it is obvious—to anyone of a controllable imagination—that his brother must be the main suspect.'

'Yes, but . . .'

'And therefore all facts need to be viewed in the light of this premise to see if they fit. The more they do, the more probable it becomes that such a solution is the correct one.'

'The Bennassar brothers also had both motive and opportunity.'

'Their motive arose only when they learned the identity of the man who'd seduced their sister. How did they learn that?'

'I don't know.'

'Why not?'

'They haven't yet gone as far as to admit they were anywhere near Ca'n Cullom on the Thursday.'

'Have you not challenged the younger brother with the evidence of the farmer who identified him from the photograph?'

'I haven't had time . . .'

'An efficient detective makes time. I have not the slightest doubt that they will tell you they received an anonymous telephone call giving them Cullom's name, the purpose of which, clearly, was to draw them to the area to be seen. In that way, if the attempt to make the death appear accidental failed, they would come under suspicion of the murder . . .'

'But señor, that's what I suggested earlier and you said I was merely complicating everything . . .'

'Kindly don't interrupt me. And I'd be grateful if you could try and learn the difference between carelessly complicating an issue and, with clear logic, elucidating it.'

'Señor, how do you logically explain the reason why the dog's throat was cut?'

'What's that?'

Alvarez repeated the question.

'What the devil are you trying to get at now?'

'If it had just been doped, then left to wake up naturally, who would have known it had been doped? That way, there was a better chance that Steven Cullom's death would be accepted as accidental.'

'Well—what is your explanation?'

'The only one I can think of is . . . You may have a little trouble in following what I'm trying to say. Steven Cullom was very proud of how fierce the dog was, as a weak man often tries to hide behind strength. When Alan Cullom first met the dog, he began to make friends with it and that annoyed Steven Cullom who then deliberately tried to make it dislike and challenge his brother.

'Now, suppose Alan Cullom didn't fully realize the part his brother played in the dog's antagonism. From his point of view, he kept trying to be friendly, the dog wouldn't reciprocate. When that happens, some people can be small-minded enough to start disliking the dog. If he murdered his brother for the money, then one must agree that he has a perverted character. In this case, might he not have been more concerned in gaining his revenge on the dog, by cutting its throat while unconscious, than remembering it would be infinitely better for him and his plan to let it regain consciousness?'

There was a silence. 'You were quite right,' said Salas, breaking this. 'I do have trouble in following what you're trying to say.'

'I'm sorry, señor. It is, perhaps, not completely clear in my own mind.'

'Very likely. However, as far as I understand you, the fact that the dog's throat was cut supports the probability that Alan Cullom murdered his brother?'

'Only if he is of that perverted a nature.'

'Is he?'

'I haven't yet been able to judge.'

'Why in the devil, then, aren't you judging that now?'

'There have been other possibilities to explore.'

'Suppose you restrict yourself merely to investigating them? It might lead to less circuitous routes.'

Alvarez sighed. 'Señor, there is also the question, was Palmer aware of his wife's affair and if he was, was he sufficiently jealous to kill the lover or to have him killed?'

'Well, was he? Or is that one more question which still requires "exploring"?'

'I cannot be certain. But from all his wife has said I believe he's the kind of man who deliberately turns a blind eye to what's going on because to do otherwise would be to puncture his self-esteem; but, if he can no longer do so, his emotions are all the more violent for having been suppressed.'

'Alvarez, do you positively enjoy complicating the simplest issue?'

'No, señor, but . . .'

'Have you ever stopped to remember that when you were being trained—always assuming you were—you were told many times that a simple explanation is more likely to be correct than a complicated one?'

'In Señor Palmer's case . . .'

'The obvious, and simplest, explanation is that his wife has managed to hide the affair from him, which is why he's never taken her to task over it. In which case, of course, he had no motive for the murder.'

'But surely one has to remember the possibility that he did have a motive?'

'I don't doubt that you will.'

'Señor, I feel I should have a word with Lady Molton to discover if she can help.'

'Very well. You can fly to Menorca tomorrow morning.'

'I was thinking of taking the ferry . . .'

'Why waste so much time?'

'I don't really like flying.'

'No, you wouldn't,' snapped Salas, before he replaced the receiver.

The Baleares were often described as if they were a group of islands with one identity. This was right in the broad sense and wrong in the narrow one. Geography was responsible for some of the differences between Mallorca and Menorca, history for others. Although Menorca lay only slightly to the east, this brought it more frequently within the consequential effects of the fierce weather which swept down from the Pyrenees; as there was no west to east range of mountains to form a barrier to winds, these swept over the whole of the island and often visitors' overriding memory of their stay was of banging shutters, lifting tiles, and permanently leaning trees. Nelson's fleet had used the ports and the British had left behind the art of making good gin, sash windows, tea-time pastries, blue eyes, and blonde hair. In the Civil War, the soldiers on Menorca had risen before the officers could act and so Menorca had declared for the Left while Mallorca was for the Right; many landowners and businessmen, rather than peasants, had disappeared. After the Civil War, there was the resentment of the vanquished and a fiercer sense of independence than in Mallorca; long before Franco's death, after which it became legal to print and teach in Menorquin, the Menorquins would often speak only Menorquin to visitors, even refusing to understand Castilian. And because of this stubborn, resentful independence, Menorca had not succumbed to the tourist invasion to the same extent as had Mallorca and their coastline and beaches were still, relatively speaking, uncrowded and beautiful.

'It's a hell of a long way,' muttered the traffic sergeant who was driving the ancient, rattling Seat 124.

'Not really . . .' began Alvarez

'It is when you were supposed to be getting home early.'

'I'm sorry if I've messed things up for you.'

'I suppose it's not really your fault,' replied the sergeant grudgingly.

Alvarez stared through the window at the fields whose crops were noticeably lighter than those grown around Llueso. Not a patch on home, he thought, with comforting certainty. They breasted a rolling rise, to the right of which was a talaiot, and the sergeant slowed the car. 'According to what I was told, the place is somewhere round here . . . We'll ask that bloke.'

A mule cart was plodding along ahead of them, the driver half asleep. The car drew alongside and the sergeant shouted to ask where Ca'n Jennet was? The muleteer summed up sufficient energy to point to a dirt track a couple of hundred metres ahead to the right, then slumped back.

Half a kilometre down the bumpy dirt track, they came in sight of a small finca, beyond which were two rows of loose boxes, enclosing a yard, and half a dozen paddocks, with post and rail fencing; there were horses in three of the paddocks.

The driver braked to a halt. 'Horses! Can't stand the bloody things.'

'Dangerous at both ends,' said Alvarez. He opened his door. 'Are you coming in?'

'No.' The driver settled deeper into the seat and closed his eyes.

Alvarez walked across the stone-chip surface clumped with weeds, and came up to the wooden front door that was grey and cracked from lack of oiling. The brass knocker, dull and dirty, was in the shape of a horse. He used it twice. It was over a minute before the door was opened.

She was taller than he and very much thinner. Her face was long and high cheekbones made it angular. Her hair, of nondescript colour, was unstyled and cut short. Her hands were large and strong, with roughened skin. He introduced himself and she studied him for quite some time before she jerked her head in the direction of the interior of the house. 'You'd better come on inside.' Her voice was deep, her manner abrupt.

They went into a room that was sparsely furnished, although on the mantelpiece over the large open fireplace there were a number of a cups and medals, all polished, and on the walls hung more than a dozen framed photographs of horses. In the far corner was a desk; the lid was down to form a working surface which appeared to be a chaos of papers and books.

'Sit down there.'

He sat at the end of the sofa which was not littered with newspapers and magazines. He reflected that she issued commands rather than invitations.

'I suppose you want something to drink?'

'There's no need, thank you . . .'

'I'd like something.' She left the room, to return with a four-litre flagon of wine and two glasses. She filled one glass and passed it to him.

The wine was sourly cheap, imported from the Peninsula in tankers; or perhaps, as some islanders claimed, it was made from chemicals.

She used a foot to push an empty cardboard box off a pouffe, then sat. There was no grace in her movements only a suggestion of whipcord strength.

'I am very sorry about Señor Steven Cullom,' he said. 'It will be a sad time for you.'

She made no acknowledgement of his commiserating words. 'Your being here means you don't think it was an accident?'

'I am afraid that we are virtually certain he was murdered.'

'Was he, indeed?'

He had come expecting to find a woman who mourned. Yet if he were to judge by her present attitude, she was indifferent to Steven Cullom's death.

'Who killed him?' she asked abruptly.

'I do not know yet.'

'It's no good expecting me to be able to help.'

'You may not know that you can, but something you tell me may enable me to identify the murderer.'

'All I can tell you is . . .' She stopped.

'Yes, señora? I am so sorry, I mean Lady Molton.'

'For God's sake!'

He couldn't decide what had aroused her sudden ire.

'I hardly knew him,' she said.

'But . . . but I've been told you were going to marry him.'

'Then you've been told more than I ever knew for certain.' She drained her glass, reached out for the flagon of wine, and refilled it. 'The first time I was on the back of a horse was my third birthday. People don't believe me when I tell them I can still remember that day perfectly, but it's true.' She looked up at the photographs hanging on the far wall. 'When I was old enough to be interested in such things, I swore I'd never marry anyone who didn't love horses as much as I did.

'Alfred loved horses, but he also loved barmaids, especially if they weren't fussy about using a whip on him. I was still young enough to find that disgusting rather than ridiculous, so I divorced him. My lawyers secured a very generous settlement—probably Alfred was scared I'd sell the story to one of the Sunday newspapers who delight in the odd quirks of the aristocracy. After me, he married number three and she stayed with him for five years. Maybe she'd discovered how to despise a man and yet go on living with him.

'I'd always loved Arabians beyond other breeds and my overriding ambition is to meld the finest lines and breed champions of champions. There's always been some wonderful blood in Spain and the cost of living used to be cheap so that's why I came here originally. Then the cost of living began to rocket and I discovered the truth of an old adage of horse breeding: you never ask yourself whether you can afford to buy a horse you want until after you've bought it.

'Things reached the stage where it began to be obvious I couldn't afford to continue as I had been. But the more I tried to accept that, the more I "knew" that my breeding policy was just about to reach fruition and so I simply had to continue. I became quite desperate. I even wrote to Alfred to ask him if he'd lend me sufficient to carry on for long enough to reach success, but of course I never received an answer.' She became silent, lost in her thoughts, her expression sad.

After a while, Alvarez said: 'What happened after that?'

'I had an invitation to stay with friends in Llueso. At that time I was still employing one man and he was very reliable, so I could leave the horses for a couple of days and not panic all the time I was away. I thought the two days' break, away from the immediate problems, might lead to an inspiration on how to save the stud. Instead of inspiration, I met Steven at a cocktail-party we went to in another house.

'I knew what kind of a man he was immediately. You don't spend your life with horses without being able to pick out the wrong 'un. But I don't think he ever knew what kind of a woman I am. He couldn't understand that when I spent every penny I'd got on the horses I wasn't hoping to make a fortune, I was searching for perfection.

'At the end of the two days I returned here and continued struggling to find a way out of all the financial troubles . . . even though it was obvious there was no way out. Then, a week or so later, he turned up; said he wanted to see the horses because he'd always liked them.' She laughed bitterly. 'You'd only to see him ever so carefully tiptoeing round a pile of dung to know that that was a lie.

'He kept returning. To begin with, I couldn't make out what he was after unless it was to buy this place for a song when I was finally forced out and then to sell it for a profit. But after a while he offered to lend me money, at no interest, to help see me through. I asked him, what the hell was he after? He made some damn silly answer and went away. He returned on the day the local feed merchant had said he wouldn't give me any more credit. You can probably imagine what kind of a state I was in. Steven drove off and when he returned he handed me a receipt for everything I owed. And that's when he said he wanted to marry me.'

She stood, walked over to the window, and looked out at the nearest paddock and watched the horses, somnolently standing in the shade of a couple of trees. 'I'm old enough to know that men publicly praise the virtues of Penelope while privately preferring the vices of Helen. And any mirror tells me I'm no Helen. So why?

'Maybe everyone's searching for what he hasn't got. I'm chasing the perfect Arab. Steven was chasing acceptance. God knows why. With his money, what the hell did it matter if there were some people who just didn't want to know him? But you can't understand other people's longings if you don't share them.

'To begin with, I treated his proposal as a sick joke, a reversal of the favourite plot of women's historical fiction— the beautiful young girl from an impoverished family being led to the bed of an old but rich man to save her parents being thrown out of their hovel. But that kind of offer is insiduously dangerous. I began to think that with his money I'd be able to expand my stud. Marriages made in cold blood never seemed to work out any worse than those supposedly made in heaven. What if he would be after every available tarty woman? They'd keep him occupied and leave me free for the horses . . . The devil doesn't need to shout, just to murmur once.

'He knew I'd begun to think seriously about the offer. Of course he realized why I'd agree, if I did, but that didn't matter to him because he'd be getting what he wanted. He became impatient and pressed me for a definite answer. But I couldn't forget how I'd been unable to live with Alfred because I'd despised him. How long would it be before I began to despise Steven? And for the first time in my life I seriously wondered if there was not a limit to the sacrifices a rational person could make in pursuit of perfection. And now that the choice is no longer there I still don't know what answer I would finally have given . . . It's a sordid little history.' She returned to the pouffe to sit once more.

'Have you ever met Alan Cullom?'

'Once. A totally different character. Probably deliberately being as opposite as he can.'

'Did he know that his brother wanted to marry you?'

'I think he must have done . . . In fact, I know he did.'

'How can you be certain?'

'I rang Steven recently, but Alan answered the phone—I'd no idea he was on the island. He asked me whether he should yet welcome me into the family. All very ironic.'

'How do you think the two brothers got on together?'

'Like most siblings. There were ups and downs, but underneath they were conscious of the very close relationship. One of the troubles was that Steven would try to play the part of a paterfamilias and not surprisingly that annoyed Alan, who then went out of his way to cause trouble.'

'Were there any rows between them since Alan Cullom returned?'

'Something obviously made the air a bit frosty. A woman, I imagine.'

'How d'you know this?'

'Steven spent over five minutes on the phone one night telling me how he was going to cut Alan out of everything.'

'What did that mean exactly?'

'Cut him out of his will, I suppose. Very Victorian. I told him not to be so damned stupid.'

He stood. 'Thank you for your help.'

'Another drink before you go?'

'Thank you, but I'm hoping to get a plane back to Palma.'

She refilled her own glass. 'I don't suppose you can understand that occasionally a person can betray herself and yet remain true to herself?'

He answered quietly: 'I am a peasant, born to love the land and the crops which grow on it. For a promise of hectares of the richest, finest soil, I might willingly marry Satan's daughter.'

She came to her feet, holding the full glass of wine in her

right hand. 'Do you know what happens to his money?'

'If we do not find a new will or wills, his brother will inherit almost everything.'

'That's as it should be. Money shouldn't go out of a family.'

He said goodbye. She murmured an answer, gazed out of the window to watch a mare amble out of the shade and into the sunshine. He knew that she was seeing a dream disappear.

CHAPTER 18

Alvarez parked just back from the front of Portals Nous and walked to the café at which he'd previously met Amadeo and Félix. He sat at an outside table and ordered a coffee and a brandy. He drank a little of the brandy, tipped the rest into the coffee. He watched the tourists pass, many of them wearing clothes that ten years before would have caused them to be warned off the streets and he was contemptuous of them for their lack of dignity.

He saw Amadeo and was glad he was coming on his own. The matter needed a cool, subtle approach and Félix was often as subtle as a bulldozer.

He shook hands, ordered two more drinks, and chatted inconsequentially, seemingly unaware of Amadeo's growing sense of tension. A waiter brought the two brandies and took away the empty glass, cup and saucer. As the waiter moved out of earshot, Amadeo said, his voice hoarse: 'What d'you want?'

'Do you remember me having the photos on your ID cards copied?'

He swallowed heavily. Was he likely to have forgotten?

'I showed the copies to a farmer who lives below Ca'n Cullom. He identified Félix.'

'That . . . that's impossible.'

'Is it?'

'He was at the hotel all day and I was at the office.'

'The last time I spoke to you, you both agreed you'd taken the day off on trumped-up excuses and spent it with a couple of married women.'

'I . . . I was forgetting. That's what we did do . . .'

'Look, Amadeo, face the facts. I've just told you, Félix was positively identified. And if the farmer's memory improves, as often happens, he'll identify you as well.'

'I swear . . .'

'Just before you swear anything, think on this. We're distant kin. That won't stop me taking you in if I decide it was you two who killed the Englishman, but it does mean that if I reckon you were in the area but you didn't kill him, I'll do everything I can to help prove your innocence. But before I can be convinced, I need to know everything, exactly as it happened.'

Amadeo finished his brandy. He kept moistening his upper lip. Alvarez waited with endless patience.

'We . . . we were there. But I swear we didn't kill him.'

'How did you learn his name?'

Amadeo's expression sharpened as hatred momentarily overcame his fears. 'I had a phone call at the office.'

'From a man or a woman?'

'A man.'

'Was he a Mallorquin?'

'No, a foreigner.'

'What did he say?'

'Just Steven Cullom, Ca'n Cullom, Santa Victoria. I thought he must be mad or drunk. But then he mentioned Beatriz.'

'Just like that?'

'With some talking, but I can't understand English.'

'You're sure it was English?'

'I know enough about how it sounds even if I don't know what it means.'

'What did you do?'

'I said as simply as I could in Spanish that I didn't understand. After a bit he said 'child' and suddenly I realized what he was getting at.'

'He said that in English?'

'No, in Spanish—niño. Only to begin with he forgot there was a tilde on the second "n" and it didn't make sense. But after a bit he remembered to pronounce it correctly.'

'And then?'

'He rang off.'

'So you'd learned the name of the man and where he'd lived. What did you do next?'

'I told Félix.'

'How did he react?'

'He said we . . .' He stopped abruptly.

'That you must find the man and kill him?'

'You know how excited he gets. But it doesn't mean anything. I calmed him down and I said what we'd got to do was to talk to the Englishman and make him understand he must marry Beatriz.'

'How did Félix take that suggestion?'

'He didn't like it, but in the end he agreed it was the only thing to do. So I phoned his hotel and said he was ill; he phoned my office and said I was ill. Then we drove to Santa Victoria.'

'Intending to do what?'

'I've just said. To make the Englishman understand.'

'And did he?'

'We never saw him . . . I swear that's the truth. We never saw him, not to speak to, that is. We were walking along and this very expensive car drove out. We guessed it must be him. If he wasn't there, there was no point in us going up to the house.'

'You must have tried again.'

Amadeo went to speak, checked the words. He looked at Alvarez, then away.

'I've got to know everything if I'm to help.'

'We . . . we returned after dark. But there was a dog near the gate and from the way it was acting there was no chance of being able to get inside the grounds.'

'You were reckoning on breaking in, then?'

'Félix . . . Well, he'd started talking crazily again and it was difficult to make him see sense. But when he saw that dog . . . He was bitten very badly by one when he was a small kid and ever since then he's been afraid of them. We decided there wasn't anything we could do and returned home.'

'What time was it when you got back?'

'I dont know . . . Maybe it was just before midnight.'

'Has either of you been back?'

'No. I mean, we read about his death in the paper. What was there to go back for?'

'What did you feel about him dying like that?'

'That it was the hand of God.'

If said by a sophisticated man, that would have sounded naïve to the point of being sardonically ridiculous. But, despite living in so changing a time, essentially neither Amadeo nor Félix was sophisticated and they still believed that sooner or later good was rewarded and evil was punished. So the fact that Amadeo had said Steven Cullom's death was by the hand of God convinced Alvarez that neither he nor his brother had had anything to do with the murder, despite the fact that there was as yet not the slightest proof of this negative.

CHAPTER 19

Alvarez drove along the winding lanes towards Ca'n Cullom. Félix and Amadeo had been drawn to the area to inculpate them if the death of Steven Cullom was ever identified as murder. Whoever had made that telephone call to Amadeo had known that Steven Cullom had had an affair with Beatriz—a fact of which even her own family had been unaware.

Palmer's wife had been having an affair with Steven Cullom. Had Palmer known this? Even if he had, it was almost impossible to visualize him committing murder. Would he have employed someone to commit it for him, knowing the risks of being betrayed or blackmailed? How could he have known about Steven Cullom's affair with Beatriz?

Since Alan Cullom had been staying in the house, he had had the greatest opportunity. There were considerable differences of character between the two brothers and they had rowed, as brothers often did, but until recently Steven had regarded the relationship with sufficient depth of feeling to leave all his money to Alan. Which suggested that he might often have boasted about his conquests to Alan, as men often did, and had mentioned Beatriz . . . Then Steven had decided to marry. In view of this he had new wills drafted in which his wife (assuming they married) was to inherit everything except for fifty thousand pounds that were to go to Alan and a further four small bequests. But then Alan had returned to Ca'n Cullom and Susan had been there and she'd been the cause of a row between the brothers; so heated that Steven had decided to cut Alan out of his wills. So Alan under the existing wills would inherit roughly eight hundred and twenty-five thousand pounds and under the new wills, which would be executed if/when the marriage was definitely to take place, either a fraction of that or nothing . . .

It was often difficult to prove whether a death was accidental or deliberate. So frequently murder was committed in the guise of accident. But a clever, far-seeing man would acknowledge that there must be occasions when an 'accident' would be correctly identified as murder and therefore he'd cover himself by trying to make

certain that if this happened someone else would become the prime suspect or suspects . . .

He reached Ca'n Cullom. Susan, wearing a towelling
swimming robe, opened the front door. She led the way
through to the pool terrace, where Alan Cullom was sunbathing. He came to his feet and faced Alvarez, his expression antagonistic and wary.

Alvarez sat under the shade of a sun umbrella set in the
middle of a metal table; when asked what he'd like to drink, he
replied, 'A brandy.' She left them and returned into the house.

Alan Cullom said belligerently: 'D'you still think Steve
was murdered and didn't just fall?'

'It has yet to be finally confirmed by the forensic evidence,
but there is no doubt that he was murdered.'

'Why should anyone have killed him?'

'He was very wealthy . . . You realized, naturally, that
your brother was very wealthy?'

'Naturally,' replied Alan Cullom sarcastically.

'His total estate is probably as much as eight hundred and
twenty-five thousand pounds . . . You are not surprised?'

'No. Steve was the kind of person who let you know . . .
But what the hell's it matter what kind of person he was?
Now he's dead, let the poor sod rest in peace.'

'Is that not a strange way in which to refer to your
brother?'

'Not if you're English. Don't you know, we conceal our
affections?'

Susan returned. She handed Alvarez a glass, then set out
two earthenware cazuelas, one containing fried almonds
and the other crisps. 'What's the trouble now, Inspector?'

Alan Cullom said: 'They're convinced Steve was murdered. And I'd say right now they're wondering if I murdered him. Am I right?'

'I have naturally had to consider such a possibility,'
replied Alvarez

'But that's being utterly ridiculous,' she said heatedly. She faced Alvarez. 'Don't you understand, they were brothers.'

Alan Cullom said: 'The Inspector will reply that fratricide has a long history, the most notable example being Cain.'

'For God's sake, stop talking like that. It's stupid. It sounds so nasty to anyone who doesn't realize how upset you really are . . . Inspector, you mustn't think he didn't like Steve. They weren't really close, as my sister and I used to be before she was married, but they were more than friends, they were brothers.'

Again and again, Alvarez thought, that phrase was repeated. They were brothers. But, as Alan Cullom had just said, brother sometimes murdered brother, often because when such a relationship turned sour emotions would be more extreme than would otherwise have been the case. 'Did you know the contents of your brother's wills?'

'He once said that he'd made me his main beneficiary.'

'Have you read either his Spanish or his English will?'

'No.'

'Even though they were among his papers in the desk in the study?'

'Look, I may be many things, but I don't go through other people's papers.'

'You knew that your brother was contemplating marriage?'

'I knew he had that crazy idea, yes.'

'Why d'you call it crazy?'

'Because if he'd tried, he couldn't have found anyone less suitable.'

'In what way?'

'Lady Molton comes from a totally different background and Steve worried himself sick about backgrounds. On top of that, she'd only one interest in life, horses. After a month, she and Steve wouldn't have been on speaking terms.'

'Did you realize that if he married he'd change his wills?'

'Of course I goddamn well did. People who marry usually do.'

'Alan,' she said pleadingly.

'All right, I'll keep it cool. But being asked a load of irrelevant questions ...'

'Perhaps, señor, their relevance will soon become more obvious ... Under his new, draft wills, your brother intended to leave you just fifty thousand pounds.'

'So?'

'You knew that?'

'He'd said at some time or other that if ever he got married again he'd make certain I'd still get something.'

'Did your brother recently threaten to cut you out altogether?'

'No.'

'María says she heard him say this.'

'She heard us arguing. Her English isn't good enough to know the details.'

'But you agree there was an argument?'

'Steve had a quick temper.'

'Why was he in a temper on this occasion?'

'I can't remember; he'd blow his top over almost anything.'

'Was it because of the señorita?'

'You can stop making bloody insinuations ...'

She said: 'Inspector, it wasn't Alan's fault. Steve thought ...'

Alan Cullom interrupted her. 'It's none of his business what Steve thought.'

'Can't you realize it is, until he can understand that you couldn't ever have killed your own brother? Oh God, why are you being so blind?'

'I don't like the family's dirty washing being laundered in public.'

'Isn't it better to launder it now, when it's not really public?' She faced Alvarez, her chin held high. 'Steve met me in Menorca and invited me here because he thought I'd jump into bed with him. I came because I was feeling miserable and was naïve enough to believe his motive had been kindness. When I refused to cooperate, he became annoyed. Then Alan arrived and was unwise enough to tell him he was making a fool of himself. That made him absolutely furious.'

'Thank you, señorita . . . So, señor, that is why he decided to cut you out of his wills?'

'I don't believe he did.'

'Shortly before he died he spoke to Lady Molton over the telephone and told her that that was what he intended to do.'

Susan said urgently: 'It doesn't mean he really meant it. Alan's told you, he had a very quick temper. But he'd get over it just as quickly.'

She remained a fighter, Alvarez thought, even when the fight became more and more hopeless. 'Señor, did you know that your brother had had an affair with a Mallorquin girl?'

'What's that?' Alan Cullom tried to direct his mind to this new line of questioning. Alvarez repeated the question. 'He once mentioned something about it.'

'Did he name her?'

'I don't remember anything except that he said she was wonderfully simple.'

He used the word "wonderfully"?'

Susan, who'd been watching Alvarez's expression, said: 'Do . . . do you know the girl?'

'She is a cousin.'

'Oh my God!'

'I'm sorry,' Alan said. 'But you can't blame me for what happened.'

'It is important to know if you were aware of the relation-ship.'

'Why?'

Alvarez gave no answer.

'Did it . . . Did it upset her very much,' Susan asked.

'She was young.' He would not now say anything more. 'Señor, may I have your permission to search your bed-room?'

'You bloody well may not.'

'Alan,' she said, 'neither of us has anything to hide. Wouldn't it be infinitely better if the Inspector searched both our rooms and found that out for himself?'

He hesitated. 'All right,' he said finally.

They left the patio and went upstairs. 'My room's there.' Susan pointed.

'I have no need to go into your room, señorita.'

'I'd much prefer it if you did.'

He searched her room, hating this unnecessary intrusion into her privacy but understanding the feelings which had prompted her to demand that he did.

'D'you enjoy looking through women's underclothes?' Alan Cullom asked crudely, as Alvarez closed the bottom drawer of the bombé commode with elaborate marquetry.

She gripped Alan Cullom's right arm. 'Please,' she said, a note of despair in her voice.

They crossed the landing and entered Alan Cullom's bedroom.

'What exactly are you looking for?' she asked.

'Among other things, señorita, the draft English will.'

Alan Cullom said scornfully: 'And you think I pinched it and it's hidden in here?'

'Perhaps.'

'Then the best of bloody British luck to you.'

Alvarez checked the few clothes hanging in the built-in cupboards, the contents of drawers, and the battered, empty holdall.

'Finally satisfied?'

'Are there any of your possessions anywhere else in the house, señor?'

'No.'

'Yes, there are,' she corrected him, determined that nothing should be overlooked. 'Your shoes which I keep meaning to try and mend.'

'I'd forgotten them. Very, very important!'

'I'd like to see them, señor.'

'I'm sure you would. Maybe the missing draft will is in one of the toes.'

They went downstairs and through the kitchen to the utility room beyond. Along one wall was a deep shelf and on this, beyond a tool box, was a pair of battered yachting shoes, the uppers of which had begun to part from the soles.

'Don't forget to look all round inside,' jeered Alan Cullom.

Alvarez turned them over. The soles consisted of countless small rounds of rubber, giving grip on a wet deck, and these allowed small objects to become impacted between them. On the corner of one sole was some soil which had been stained. He remembered the slight impression near the dead man's head in the bloodstained soil.

He drove slowly to Santa Victoria. The shoes must be sent to the forensic laboratory, together with the soil samples he'd just secured. He had no doubt that the results of tests would show that the two soils were similar and that the stains would prove to be of human blood, of the same group as that of the dead man's. He wondered about the draft will. Had Alan Cullom destroyed it, hoping that this would prevent its existence becoming known? But weren't the odds against that? The Spanish solicitor had drafted a fresh will and therefore it would be reasonable to suppose that the English solicitors had done the same. No, surely he would have decided to hold on to the draft because it might provide him with 'an alibi of motive'. Initially, he'd set the scene to look like accidental death. He'd hoped the authorities would accept it as that, but he'd been clever enough to realize that they might not and then they'd indentify persons with a motive for committing murder. He'd drawn Amadeo and Félix to the area; they had reason for wishing Steven Cullom dead. But then he'd been realistic as well as clever and had gone on to accept that even with two prime suspects, the police would still be very much aware of the fact that he had an equally strong motive. So he needed something to ease the pressure if ever it became at all dangerous. The draft will showed that he was still to inherit fifty thousand pounds, a large enough sum to negate his motive . . . He wasn't to know that his brother would tell Lady Molton that he was going to cut him right out . . .

The draft will had not been in the study or the bedroom. If it were hidden anywhere else in the house, there'd always be the chance that someone would accidentally find it: and once found it would have to be disclosed to the police immediately and not be held back for the right psychological moment . . . Where could Alan Cullom have hidden the draft so that he could be certain it was secure and yet be available the moment he wanted it? . . .

The post office was in a side street, tucked anonymously and contiguously between two houses. Inside was a small public area, with very well worn tiles, and at the far end of this were two counters, the left-hand one of which was always kept closed because the staff did not like to be rushed.

Alvarez identified himself. The post office worker behind the counter regarded him with a wary dislike.

'I'm looking for a letter. I don't know what size it is, who it's addressed to, or when it was posted.'

'Isn't there anything else you don't know about it?'

'I can probably think of something if you'd like? . . . Will you go through all the mail in hand?'

'And find a letter which you won't know when you see it? . . . You'd better come through and start looking. I'm not going to waste my time. Too much else to do.'

Alvarez went through a doorway and round behind the counter. Fixed to the wall were a series of cubbyholes, designated by the letters of the alphabet.

It was ten minutes after he'd started work, when he'd

reached the E cubbyhole, that he picked up a long white envelope of a size which would, he judged, accommodate a document like the English will he had seen. He checked the typewritten name and address; Alan Ernest, Lista de correos, Santa Victoria.

Alan Cullom said: 'What the hell is it this time?'

'First,' replied Alvarez, 'I need to know whether you have another christian name?'

'What if I have?'

'Alan,' said Susan in a low voice.

He jammed his hands in the pockets of the shorts he was now wearing and he stared bitterly at Alvarez across the air-conditioned sitting-room. 'We're on our way out for a meal.'

'I shan't keep you long.'

'Anything to prove you right ... My second name's Ernest.'

'There is, I remember, a typewriter in the study. I intend to use it.'

'Why?'

'I need a sample of its type.'

'At the risk of becoming monotonous, why?'

'I have just recovered from the post office in Santa Victoria a letter addressed to Alan Ernest. Inside the envelope was the draft English will of your brother.'

Alan Cullom's expression was shocked; Susan's was one of growing despair.

Alvarez left the sitting-room and crossed the hall to go into the study. The typewriter stood on a small table behind and to the right of the desk. He removed the cover, fed in a plain sheet of paper, and typed. He removed the paper and compared the typeface with that on the envelope. Superficially, they were similar. He didn't doubt that an expert examination would show they were identical. He replaced the typewriter cover.

Back in the sitting-room Susan, her face flushed, was standing by the side of Alan Cullom's chair.

Alvarez said: 'Will you please give me your passport. And understand that you are not to leave this island until you are given permission to do so.'

'I didn't kill Steve,' said Alan Cullom hoarsely.

'Your passport?'

'You bloody fool,' he shouted, 'you don't begin to understand a thing.' He stood, so suddenly that Susan's hand was jerked upwards before she had time to release her grip. He left the room. Susan stared at Alvarez and seemed to be about to say something, then she too hurried out.

Alan Cullom returned, alone, and handed over his passport. 'I did not kill him,' he said violently.

Alvarez had left the house and was just about to climb into his car when the sound of his name checked him. He turned to see Susan. She hurried over to where he stood. 'You've got to listen to me,' she said desperately.

'Señorita, there is nothing I can do because I cannot change the facts.'

'It wouldn't have mattered what happened, he couldn't have done anything to hurt Steven.'

He wished the sight of her distress did not squeeze his emotions. 'Someone killed his brother.'

'But it wasn't Alan. Please, please believe me.'

'I have to judge the facts . . .'

'Oh God, you won't understand a word I'm saying.' Her face worked as if she were crying, but there were as yet no tears. 'It doesn't matter what anyone says, Alan couldn't have killed Steven.'

'But the evidence . . .'

'Why won't you believe me?'

'Señorita, the evidence is too definite.'

Tears finally spilled down her cheeks. Desperation and grief made her appear almost ugly. She turned and ran into the house.

CHAPTER 20

The forensic laboratory telephoned on Friday morning. An assistant reported that the two samples of earth were similar in all respects, that the on-site sample contained traces of human blood, and that the blood had been typed and was the same as that of the dead man's.

Alvarez replaced the receiver. He stared at the shaft of brilliant sunshine coming through the opened window in which a myriad dust particles danced. That was near-conclusive proof. The final, conclusive proof lay in the top left-hand drawer of the desk. He opened the drawer and stared at the envelope which contained the draft English will. Then he slammed the drawer shut.

He reached down to the bottom right-hand drawer and brought out of it the brandy and the glass.

Kitchen work was a woman's job and although Dolores often complained that she had to slave from morning to night, she accepted as natural the fact that while she was doing the washing-up, the men should be doing nothing more strenuous than drinking; indeed, in a strange way, she would have been quite indignant had they tried to help her, judging this to be an implied slur on her capabilities as a good housewife . . . and also on their standing as men. So when, as she stood at the sink, she heard someone enter the kitchen after lunch, she snapped: 'What do you want?'

'I . . .'

She turned to see Alvarez. 'Well?'

He came right inside.

'Are you ill?'

'Of course not.'

'Then maybe you'll say what you've got to say and leave

me to do the work.' She turned back, lifted a glass out of the soapy water, and put it in the rinsing water.

He crossed to the centre table and began to play with a knife, spinning it round on a plate.

'I can manage without you carrying on like that.'

'Dolores . . .'

His tone finally alerted her. She once more faced him. 'Enrique, what's up?'

'I'm in one hell of a situation. I know what I ought to do, but I just can't bring myself to do it.'

'This has to do with those women?'

'In a way. But you must understand, it's not like you think.'

'Are you certain you're not making a fool of yourself?'

'Why won't you recognize that a man can just admire a woman?'

'Because I've never met one who stopped at that.' The moment she'd finished speaking, she swore at herself for letting her tongue run unchecked. She said hastily: 'Enrique, tell me what the trouble is.'

'I had a phone call from Palma this morning.' He began to fidget with the knife again. 'It virtually confirms the fact that the man she loves murdered his brother. I've held back one further piece of evidence which quite definitely does confirm it.'

'But . . . but you shouldn't have done that, should you?'

'Of course I shouldn't. But if I pass it on, he'll be arrested. And that'll break her.'

Dear God, she thought, why had he chosen a job which was forever stretching his emotions? 'What will happen if you continue not to tell the superior chief about this evidence? I mean, as far as you're concerned?'

'I suppose there'll be no arrest. He'll just think I've been my usual incompetent self.'

'And what if somehow he learns you've kept it from him?'

'I'll be sacked.'

'Enrique, you can't risk so much for this woman.'

Logically, she was right; morally, she was right. But she had never looked into those dark blue eyes and seen their capacity for hurt . . .

He lay on his bed and for once he could not sleep.

Had he missed something, somewhere? Yet since Steven Cullom had died before he executed the second English will, no one but Alan stood to gain financially from his death. Then, despite the fortune at stake, had the motive really been jealousy or revenge? Another woman seduced, abandoned? This was the only alternative. Never mind all the questions that such a solution raised. Assume he had been murdered for love, not money; then somewhere there had to be a woman who had planned and plotted . . . How to identify her? How to single out one woman from all those a man with money and an unbridled passion had seduced? Among his papers there was no diary, recording in salacious details his conquests . . . Amelia Hart, he thought suddenly. Often a man was unable to keep all his infamy to himself, needing to confess—often in the form of boasting; as he had boasted to her—as if by confessing he divested himself of some iniquity. She might know of another woman whose husband was of a far stronger character than Palmer . . .

Amelia and her husband were sitting out on the patio, under the shade of the overhead vines. Hart said: 'Excellent timing! I'm just about to go inside and pour out the drinks.'

'Then I am sorry to have arrived at such a moment, señor.'

'You're the first person out here I've ever heard apologize on that score! Come and sit down.'

'How's the world treating you?' asked Amelia from her wheelchair as Alvarez sat.

'Not very generously, señora.'

'I must say, you look as if you'd all the cares of the world on your shoulders. Relax and forget them. When I was a child I had a nursemaid who was always telling me not to worry because nothing was ever quite as bad as it was imagined to be.'

'Only true if you're of small imagination,' said Hart.

'Will you please stop being cynical and find out what our guest would like to drink.'

'A brandy, señora, please.'

'With ice, but no soda . . . Isn't that right?'

'Exactly right.'

'There you are, Pat!' she exclaimed. 'And you have the nerve to tell me I have a poor memory.'

'Not poor, hopeless.'

'Look who's talking! Only yesterday I asked you to get me a bar of that gorgeous Côte d'Or chocolate and you didn't.'

'And you're now forgetting that the doctor said you had to cut back on sugar.'

'Are you admitting you didn't forget, you deliberately didn't buy it?'

He smiled, then went inside the house.

'Husbands! I'm sure a little chocolate would have done me far more good than harm, whatever that misery of a doctor said.' She studied Alvarez, then spoke with her usual directness. 'I suppose you're here again because of Steven?'

'I'm afraid so.'

'The local gossips are having a field day and saying that Alan killed him. I had a hell of a row with one yesterday and called her a couple of names no lady should even know . . . You realize it couldn't possibly have been Alan, don't you? He can be very difficult, especially when he's in one of his moods, and there were plenty of rows between them, mainly because Steve thought so much of established values, but brothers so often carry on like that. And considering they were only half-brothers, they really got on very well together.'

Hart returned with a tray on which were three glasses

that were already frosting. He handed them around, sat. Amelia rested her glass on her lap. 'The Inspector's come to have a chat about Steven.'

'Frankly, I didn't imagine it was because he found us socially irresistible . . . So, Inspector, how's the case going?'

'It is very difficult, señor.'

'I imagine it must be. Though not if you listen to local gossip.'

'I've already told him the old hens are having a field day,' said Amelia.

'Nothing better to talk about and nothing to think with even if they had. How the hell can anyone with an ounce of understanding imagine for a second that Alan could murder his own brother?'

Alvarez knew a quick moment of pleasure that there were at least two people with a sense of loyalty. 'I must ask you some more questions, señora. I am very sorry if they upset you, or perhaps even offend you, but you once told me that Señor Steven Cullom used to confide in you?'

'That's right.'

'And he mentioned his affairs with women?'

'Some of them, at least.' She sighed. 'It was all rather pathetic. He went out of his way to tell me what a Don Juan he was, but I'm certain he never realized that essentially Don Juan was a figure of tragedy. Of course, all the boasting was probably concealing some character or physical defect in himself.'

'What kind of defect?'

'That's anybody's guess. But if you ask me, I'd say it was trying to compensate for the fact that quite a lot of people didn't like him. But it could equally have been homosexual tendencies or trying to prove he was the world's greatest lover because a woman had once told him he was hopeless in bed.'

'I don't think he was lying all that much,' said Hart, 'and I don't go for arcane explanations. I reckon he was just

plain randy. So with his money it's quite possible he did
have a whole succession of women.'

'Spoken like a true male chauvinist pig! Convinced that
all you need to do is offer any woman enough and she'll lie
down.'

'My wife,' Hart said, 'has a low opinion of men and a
high opinion of women.'

'With good reason,' she said. 'But let's not develop that
theme or the Inspector will think I'm as sour as the wine
we were given the other evening.'

'I could never begin to think of you as sour,' Alvarez
said.

'You really mean that? I told you, when we first met, that
we are truly sympathetic towards each other.'

'What is this?' asked Hart, 'a mutual admiration
society?'

'You, sir, are a cynical old man who can't recognize
sincerity when you meet it.'

'Perhaps it's so long ago when I last did that I've forgotten
what it looks like.'

'Thank you very much.' She said to Alvarez: 'I do hope
you can understand the British sense of humour?'

'No, señora, I cannot. But I can recognize it.'

'I rather like that, especially the inference with which I
thoroughly agree. It's far too often too close to unkindness
to be in the least bit genuinely amusing.'

'Someone once said that all humour was based on misfortune,' said Hart.

'And that someone was pompous, self-satisfied, and
totally wrong.'

'So now we know.'

'So now you know.'

Alvarez said: 'Señora, did he name the women he had
met?'

'Only by their christian names and sometimes not even
by them.'

'Did he ever mention a woman who was married, apart from Señora Palmer?'

'I don't think so. A married woman entailed risk and that wasn't to his liking. He once told me that package fortnight holidays were the greatest invention of the twentieth century. It gave the women one day to warm up, twelve days of heat, and one day to cool down.'

'Was he ever threatened because of an affair he'd had?'

'He certainly never mentioned anything like that.'

'But he could have been having an affair with a married woman and you wouldn't have known about it?'

'Of course.'

Gloomily, Alvarez thought that despite the last answer there was now no room left for evasion; almost certainly there had not been an angry husband determined to avenge his wife's adultery . . .

'I've not been able to help you, have I?' she asked.

'No, señora, I'm afraid not.'

'Does that mean that Alan . . .' She stopped.

'Can you possibly tell us,' asked Hart, 'is there any truth in the suggestion that Alan is under suspicion?'

'I think the only answer I can give you, señor, is that until I know more than I do now, everyone who is in any way directly connected with the dead man is under suspicion.'

'Yes, I suppose they must be. But Alan . . .' He shook his head.

She spoke with a sudden bitterness. 'You know what it is, don't you? It's the curse, working its way through the family.'

'For heaven's sake!'

'You can't just sit there and say for heaven's sake and blow it all away.'

'There's nothing to blow away.' He turned to Alvarez. 'Amelia's normally the most realistic of people, but she's been very upset by this business and for the first time since we married she's become superstitious.'

'You have to admit . . .'

'I admit that several unfortunate things have happened to the family over the past eighteen months. But they're coincidences.'

'They are not.'

'Just as in the case of Tutankhamun's tomb, which you quoted to me yesterday, if you take the trouble to study the evidence you'll find there was no trail of connected tragedies bearing out the curse, they either didn't happen as the myth tries to make out they did or they were isolated events which had no bearing on or relation to each other.'

'How d'you know that what you say's right? How can you say so categorically whether the events were isolated or connected?'

'Because I don't accept predestination. Apart from anything else, if you accept it you stop fighting . . .'

'Have I ever stopped fighting?'

'No, of course you haven't. Until now you've always had a logical outlook on life. But accept there's a curse on the Culloms and you're accepting predestination; accept that, and although you may consciously go on fighting, subconsciously . . .'

'There's more drivel talked about the subconscious than anything else. Determine to fight and you'll go on fighting. Accepting facts won't alter that.'

'Here, there are no facts to accept.'

'But you know there are. Last year, Basil was killed in a car accident. In February, both of us could so easily have been killed when the brakes failed in the car. Steven's been murdered. Alan is suspected . . . Out of four sets of cousins, three have met trouble. Can you really claim that's just coincidence?'

'I refuse to believe that some dark force has laid a curse on the Culloms. That's against all reason, logic, and common sense.'

She stared at him, her expression deeply worried. 'I wish to God I possessed your certainty that the world is ruled by reason, logic, and common sense. But being confined to a wheelchair when nearly everyone else is walking about makes me believe that the world's illogical and desperately unfair. And that's why I can believe in a dark force and a curse on a family . . . I'm sorry.' she said to Alvarez. 'It's been awful, having to listen to all that. But sometimes I have a bad day and some of the black shadows come out of hiding . . . But you can understand, can't you?'

'I can understand,' he answered.

CHAPTER 21

As Alvarez sat behind his desk, Amelia's words kept running through his mind. The curse of the Culloms. Four sets of cousins, of which three had suffered tragedies or near-tragedies; five cousins, four of whom had been affected. Coincidence, as Hart had declared? Wasn't that taking coincidence too far? A curse, as Amelia feared? In the last quarter of the twentieth century, could anyone really believe in the power of a curse?

He lifted his feet and put them on the desk, his heels resting on the unopened mail which had arrived that morning. He believed in God, therefore he must believe in the devil; he believed in goodness, therefore he must believe in evil; he believed that some families enjoyed unusual fortune, therefore he must believe that some families must suffer unusual misfortune; but he simply could not believe that a curse could be laid on five cousins, perhaps because his faith was not sufficiently strong.

If there were no curse and events were not to be explained by coincidence, what then? Especially remembering that there were eight hundred and twenty-five thousand pounds at stake . . .

For the moment, accept that the murderer was not Alan Cullom. Then one had to postulate a murderer who had set out to make it appear initially that the death had been an accident, then that it would seem to be a murder and the two Bennassar brothers would be suspected. But certain carefully planted inconsistencies would gradually suggest that they had deliberately been drawn to the scene in order to conceal the fact that the murderer had really been Alan Cullom . . .

That telephone call which Susan had heard—or had she? —in the middle of the night on which Steven Cullom had been killed. That must have been to lure him outside the house; perhaps the caller had said he'd evidence that the two brothers knew about Steven Cullom's seduction of their sister and they had been looking for him . . . Alan couldn't have made the call from the house because there were just the main phone and an extension and when one lifted the first, one could not call the second . . .

Only two motives had come to light. Women and money. Why would an outraged husband seek his revenge in so roundabout and complicated a fashion? If Alan had been falsely inculpated, why—when only he stood to benefit financially to any extent from his brother's death? . . .

The telephone disturbed Alvarez's laboured thoughts. Superior Chief Salas said: 'I've had no report from you. What the devil's going on?'

'I've had a number of inquiries to make . . .'

'Have you made them?'

'Yes, señor.'

'With what result?'

'To tell the truth, they seem only to confuse the issue.'

'Was there, then, room for further confusion? . . . I understand you've received a report from Forensic?'

'Yes, señor.'

'I wonder if it will in any way disturb you to learn that I only became aware of this fact in the course of a conversation with someone from that department on other matters?'

'I was just about to ring and inform you.'

'Then I should feel grateful for that much. Have you arrested Alan Cullom?'

'No, señor.'

'Why not?'

'There is some further evidence which I decided I must check out first.'

'Then you do not consider that the evidence from the forensic laboratory is conclusive?'

'Not really, no.'

'What is this fresh evidence?'

'The fact that there were five Cullom cousins and out of the five, two are dead and two others are, or have been, in trouble. I'm wondering about the curse of the Culloms . . .'

'What's that?'

'The curse of the Culloms, señor.'

'Are you by any chance drunk?'

'Certainly not. I was going to add that I don't believe in that kind of a curse. But neither do I believe in extreme coincidences. That's why I would like permission to travel to England.'

'You'd like to go to England. Aren't you just back from Menorca?'

'Yes, but . . .'

'You don't think that maybe you are mistaking this office for that of a travel agency?'

'Señor, the truth has to be somewhere and I think only England can explain to me exactly where. Perhaps I could telephone and speak to someone over there and ask him to find the answers to certain questions, but the subject is . . . well, not easily definable. He might not readily be able to understand what I'm after.'

'I agree.'

'But if I meet someone and we get to know each other, I can give him the full background to the case. Then he'll understand why I need to know who, apart from Alan Cullom, could possibly stand to benefit from the murder of two Culloms and the harassment of others.'

'Did you say the murder of *two* Culloms?'

'Basil Cullom died last year.'

'And it is established that he was murdered?'

'Not established, no. After all, as yet I haven't any details on his death. But he must have been murdered because everything points to that.'

'Do you realize that you've joined certain events together, quite careless of the fact that there's not the slightest evidence there's any direct connection between them, and from this bastard union you've drawn a highly contentious conclusion? Now, you are trying to offer this conclusion as not only proof that the facts were rightly joined together in the first place, but also as proof of something which I can only describe as an extraordinary flight of the imagination.'

Alvarez rubbed the sweat from his forehead with the back of his hand. Was that what he was doing?

'Do you wish to reconsider all you've told me?'

'Not really, señor. You see, I think I'm right.'

'And, no doubt, you put forward such conviction as proof of the facts on which you're relying?'

'Señor, I'm certain the answer lies in England. That's why I want to have your permission to go there.'

'Unfortunately I am bound, since you are the investigating officer, to accede to any reasonable request. The fact that your definition of "reasonable" differs so greatly from mine is not allowed to bear the due weight it should. Regretfully, I have to agree to your going.'

The flight on Monday was one that Alvarez would never forget. Halfway through, when the first of the lunch trays was being collected, there was an announcement over the speaker system asking passengers to fasten their seat-belts as there was the possibility of turbulence ahead. For ten minutes nothing happened. Then, with not even a preliminary lurch, the plane had—at least, in his fevered imagination—looped-the-loop, performed a couple of Immelmann turns, and cartwheeled across the sky like a fourteen-year-old in the Olympic gymnastics. When it was finally over, he didn't praise the designers and builders who'd put such strength into the plane, he cursed them. In a trembling voice, he called for a double brandy. The air hostess who brought it said, in her calm-the-passenger voice, that that had been rather fun, hadn't it? For the first time in his life, he was sorely tempted to strike a woman.

They arrived at Heathrow, this being an Iberia flight, and such was the measure of what he'd already been through that the actual landing caused him no further distress.

He'd been booked into a small hotel, run by Spaniards from Galicia, which was in South Kensington and catered exclusively for package tours from Spain. The husband, his manner polite but cold, showed him to his room; the husband had left Spain many years before, when the police were to be feared and avoided at all costs.

Alvarez washed his face in the handbasin, then crossed to the window and looked out. It had recently been raining heavily and the road was glistening and the heavy traffic was throwing up dirty spray; pedestrians were wearing mackintoshes or carrying umbrellas. Although it was barely six hours since he'd stepped out of the house in Calle Juan Rives into harsh sunshine, he knew a sudden and bitter homesickness.

Detective-Sergeant Jennings arrived at the hotel at a quarter to five and they settled in the small reading-room that was otherwise empty. He offered a pack of Senior Service. 'I hope we can help you on this one,' he said, as he held out a lighter. He was a tall, rangy man, with a round face in which were lines of humour. 'But frankly, I'm not quite clear what it is you're after?'

'I have to confess, señor, that no more am I.'

'Then we're off to a good start!' Jennings's smile robbed the words of any possible offence.

A waiter entered and, in Spanish, asked them if they'd like anything; Alvarez ordered coffee. Then, when they were once more on their own, he gave a brief résumé of the Cullom case. The waiter returned with coffee and rather sickly-looking individual cakes as Alvarez finished speaking.

Jennings poured himself a coffee after filling Alvarez's cup. 'It's all ifs and buts, isn't it?'

'I am afraid so.'

'But as you say, the point to start at is the accident to Basil Cullom last year. Have you a note of his address, whether he was married, and the date of the crash?'

'He was married, but he'd no children.' Alvarez brought a notebook out of the pocket of his coat and opened it. 'He lived at Brecton Cottage, Astonwater, near Keswick. I've spoken to Amelia Hart and she says that his widow has continued to live there after his death.'

'And the date of the crash?'

'I can't say any more exactly than that it was about the beginning of March of last year.'

'That should be good enough.' Jennings finished writing and looked up. 'And you think it wasn't a straight accidental crash?'

'I know nothing for certain. Amelia Hart says he lived up a fairly steep hill and something went wrong with the car when he was driving down. She and her husband very nearly crashed in Mallorca in February of this year when the brakes of their car failed on a hill. The owner of the garage where the car was repaired called me in because he reckoned the brake line might have been sabotaged. At the time, the Harts said that that was impossible. But . . .'

'But now you're thinking that this is the kind of coincidence that stinks!'

Tuesday was a cloudy day, but at least there was no rain. Alvarez walked out of the hotel at half past ten the following morning and took the tube to Tower Hill. There was a long queue to enter the Tower of London; left to himself, he would have turned back, but Dolores had been quite definite. For years and years she had longed to visit the Tower of London, walk across London Bridge, and stand outside Buckingham Palace. Since she believed she would never have the chance to do any of those things, he was to do them for her and then report to her every last detail.

Two and half hours later he left, limping slightly and his right hip sore from the careless charge of an eight-year-old with a pointed parcel. Halfway up the slightly rising road was a free seat and gratefully he settled on it. He stared across the road at a crowd of children around an ice-cream stall. All bridges were, he decided, basically the same and therefore there was no need actually to walk across London Bridge to describe what it was like to walk across it. And Buckingham Palace could be viewed just as clearly from the inside of a taxi as from the pavement . . .

He wondered how far away was the nearest pub and whether the unbelievable laws allowed it to serve drinks at this time of day?

Jennings telephoned the hotel at nine the next morning and expressed relief at catching Alvarez before he left: Alvarez did not bother to mention that he was still in bed.

'I've some news, but rather than give it to you right now I'd like to come along to the hotel to discuss it. OK if I arrive in about half an hour?'

The reading-room was empty and they went in there again.

'I had a word with an opposite number in the Cumbrian

force,' Jennings said, 'and asked him to make a few discreet inquiries. He got back on to me earlier this morning. Basil Cullom owned an old Ford and according to his garage there was quite a problem in getting it through its last test. In fact, they advised him to buy a new one, but he said he couldn't afford to.

'His house is halfway up a fair-sized hill. The road's steep and there's a right-hand bend that's sharp. He left home on the way to work, drove off down the hill and failed to take the bend. It's only a minor road, serving half a dozen houses in all, and there was no efficient barrier except on the actual apex of the bend, and even then it wasn't a strong one. Off the road there's a slope which soon becomes precipitous. He wasn't wearing the seat-belt and the car slammed into a boulder at the bottom. Death was instantaneous.

'The question of insurance arose and the insurance company demanded a mechanical inspection of the wreck. If you ask me, they hoped they'd discover that the last test had been fudged and the car hadn't been roadworthy, freeing them from all responsibility. Anyway, the car was checked and it was discovered that the brakes were defective. But it wasn't wear and tear, it was a fractured brake line. There was doubt about the cause and the police were called in. They made inquiries, but these convinced them that as there was no known reason for anyone to have sabotaged the car, and as the fault could have been caused by a sharp stone thrown up by a front tyre, the cause of the failure was accidental. That was that. The insurance company had to pay up.'

'The facts are the same!' said Alvarez, his voice excited. 'Now there are too many coincidences, even for my superior chief.'

His excitement was replaced by familiar bewilderment. 'But why murder Basil Cullom? What is to be gained by his death? Or do we have one cousin so filled with hate and envy that he's blindly killing or wrecking the lives of his other cousins?'

'Could it be that?'

'No. I'm sure it couldn't. They didn't like each other—Amelia Hart was an exception—but surely none of them could be so stupid? No!' He slammed his hand down on the table. He failed to note Jennings's quick smile. 'The motive is the money.'

'But you told me that under the existing will that virtually all goes to Alan Cullom; while under the draft will, never executed, it would all have gone to the wife-to-be.'

'Which makes it ridiculous, unless Alan Cullom is the murderer of Steven. But if he is, why murder Basil? Why try and murder Amelia?'

'A man who murders his brother, even where that sort of money is concerned, surely has to be round the bend in the ordinary sense of the word? If so, maybe he's working off his spite even though doing so isn't to his financial advantage in every case. Are you so certain that Alan Cullom didn't murder his brother?'

'Yes.' But was he? How far had emotion submerged logic? He didn't know. He wouldn't let himself know.

'I've been having a think or two.' Jennings paused, then said: 'Something began to stir at the back of my mind.'

'What kind of something?'

'I'd rather not answer that directly because I could be so hopelessly wrong. But what I suggest is that we go along now to my place and have a word with a bloke there who's a legal pundit as well as a copper. He might be able to tell us if there is anything in the idea.'

They left the hotel and went by taxi to the modern slab concrete and glass building which now housed Scotland Yard. A lift took them up to the ninth floor and a short walk brought them to an office in which were three desks, a couple of filing cabinets, and a large bookcase filled with text books. Only one man was present and Jennings introduced him. Inspector Wheeldon.

They placed two chairs in front of the centre desk, then

sat. Jennings said: 'Inspector Alvarez has come along with
a load of facts that obviously point to something, but neither
of us can work out what. I thought you might be able to
help, sir.'

'I very much doubt it,' replied Wheeldon with cheerful
pessimism. 'But let's find out.'

Alvarez detailed concisely all that had happened. At the
conclusion, Wheeldon laced his fingers together and then
revolved his thumbs around each other. He smiled briefly.
'Couldn't you add a few more complications?'

'Señor,' began Alvarez, 'I am very sorry . . .'

'No need to be. As a matter of fact, I rather go for
something like this instead of the usual trouble where the
facts are banal and the law's obvious. Tell me something:
just how certain are you that Alan Cullom is not guilty of
murdering his brother?'

'I am positive. But as I've just said, the evidence seems
to point conclusively to his guilt.'

Wheeldon abruptly unlocked his hands, swivelled the
chair round, and reached out to open the right-hand door
of the bookcase. He brought out a book, laid this down on
the desk, checked the index, found the page he wanted. He
read for a few minutes and as he did so he hummed. He
brought out a second book and consulted that. The hum-
ming rose, then stopped abruptly as he sat back. 'I can offer
a solution. How valid it is depends on the answers to one
or two questions . . . In this country we have a law, common
I believe to many countries, which lays it down that a person
convicted of a crime may not be allowed to enjoy the fruits
of that crime. In this case, if Alan Cullom is convicted of
murdering his brother, he will not be allowed to inherit
under his brother's will.

'When a bequest fails in this manner, unless there is a
clause which covers the eventuality, the testator is held to
have died intestate as to that amount. Apart from the
bequests to charity, then, the whole of Steven Cullom's

English estate will be held to be subject to the rules of intestacy.

'These rules are quite clear. The order of succession is, surviving spouse, children, father or mother, brothers and sisters of the whole blood, brothers and sisters of the half blood, grandparents, uncles and aunts of the whole blood, and so on.' He said to Alvarez: 'Now, you've said that Steven Cullom's wife died some time ago. At the time of his death was he survived by children, parents, brothers and sisters other than Alan, grandparents, or aunts and uncles?'

'He had no children and his parents died before his wife. Alan was his sole brother. His only other living relations were his cousins.'

'That's clear enough. Referring back to the laws governing succession under intestacy, persons lose their right to inherit unless they or their issue survive the intestate and reach the age of eighteen. Succession then is *per stirpes*, which means inheritance by family, not *per caput*.

'Summing up, if Alan is found guilty of murder, Steven's wealth will be shared out among those of his cousins who were alive at his death.'

Alvarez knew that faith, not reason, had been correct.

CHAPTER 22

The house was in a row of semi-detacheds, each with a tiny front garden and a slightly larger back one. Some had garages, some didn't; they'd been built at a time when car ownership had still been confined to those who were, relatively speaking, reasonably well off. No. 14 differed from its neighbours only in that it had had a garage and this had been altered to provide a further bedroom.

Edith Ackroyd had a long, thin, angular face and a long, thin body. It was difficult to imagine that even in the first bloom of her youth she'd been physically attractive, but the warmth of her character was unmistakable. 'Maurice? He's not back from work for lunch, yet, but he shouldn't be long.' She looked curiously at them. 'Would you like to wait?'

'If we may, Mrs Ackroyd,' said Mather, the detective-constable from the local force who'd driven Alvarez out from the centre of Oxford.

'Then come along into the sitting-room. I'm sorry, but you'll have to excuse the mess; I haven't yet got round to tidying it up. We've four children at school and getting them off, shopping, and preparing lunch for Maurice who comes back every day, takes up so much time that it's quite often the afternoon before I get around to tidying the house.' Her tone suggested she wouldn't have it any other way.

The sitting-room was clean but certainly untidy. Pages from a newspaper were lying on the sofa, four magazines straddled the floor, the *TV Times* was draped over the top of the TV set, an empty beer can was on the mantelpiece, and a radio cassette, with several tapes heaped up at its side, was on a small table on which were also a couple of opened paperbacks.

'I don't know,' she said. 'My family can turn a room into a bear garden in no time flat.' She began to collect up the pages of the newspaper.

'It doesn't look like your kids can match up to mine,' said the detective-constable. 'When I sat down last night I collected a half-eaten toffee which the youngest had spat out when he got fed up with it. Took the wife quite a time to clean my trousers.'

'Ours have got past that stage, thank goodness. But I do keep remembering a friend who said that the older they get, the more trouble they become.'

'Don't let my wife hear that. The only thing that's keeping her going at the moment is the thought that one of 'em will be off to school shortly.'

Edith put the newspaper and magazines down on the

table after stacking the cassettes and closing the paperbacks. 'Do sit down, now there's a little room.' She saw the beer can and hurried over, picked it up from the mantelpiece. 'If I've said it once, I've said it a dozen times, beer cans belong in the dustbin. There's nothing looks so sordid the next morning.'

They heard the click of the front gate.

'That must be Maurice now.' She left the room, closing the door behind her.

A couple of minutes later, Ackroyd entered the sitting-room. 'I gather you're the law and you'd like a word about something?' he said cheerfully.

'That's right. I'm Detective-Constable Mather and this is Inspector Alvarez, from Mallorca.'

'From Mallorca? You're a long way from home! . . . Something to do with Steve?'

'Yes, señor.'

'Amelia rang to say things seemed to be becoming compli-cated.' He paused, then said: 'What exactly has brought you over?'

'It was not an accident.'

'Does that mean he was definitely murdered?'

'Yes, señor.'

'Good God! . . . Who the hell would have done a thing like that?'

'I am hoping you will be able to help me answer that. You knew him well?'

'No, I didn't.'

'Even though you were cousins?'

'We don't keep the same tight relationships that you do. And in any case . . . Well, the hard fact is that the Cullom cousins, with one exception, just didn't get on together. Amelia's the exception. You've probably met her?'

'Yes, several times.'

'She's an astonishing woman, as you may have realized. Every time I see her, I understand that all the things I normally worry about—taxes, rates, the mortgage—really aren't of the slightest account.' He smiled sardonically. 'Of course, such a mood of non-self doesn't long survive my goodbye to her and soon I'm back with the taxes, rates, and mortgage ... Anyway, all that aside, she's managed to be friendly with the rest of us which is quite some feat. I call her the St Francis of go-betweens.'

'You did not meet Steven Cullom very often?'

'Perhaps three times in the past ten years. He didn't even come to our wedding. And, of course, when he became so wealthy he entered a different plane and no longer knew we existed.' He tried to speak with a sense of mocking humour, but his bitterness became obvious.

'You have recently been to Mallorca?'

'That's quite right. Amelia, bless her heart, asked me out again and Edith, may she go straight to heaven but not for a long time yet, said she'd cope with the family on her own for a week.'

'Did you visit the señor's house at Santa Victoria?'

'Amelia insisted we all ought to meet and rang Steve to try to arrange something. Thankfully, he made some ridiculous excuse. We did see each other at a cocktail-party, but we carefully didn't get near enough to have to speak.'

'When was your previous visit to Mallorca?'

'That was back in January. Amelia had been been lent the house by Steve—probably to prove he'd got two houses —and she said to have a week with them. I went on my own, of course. With four kids to bring up, there's no way we can have a holiday together unless we go camping ... Look, why all these questions about what I've been doing?'

'I will explain in a minute. Are you a very skilful driver?'

'A what? Well, I suppose I'm no worse than the next man.'

'Did you realize that Steven Cullom was wealthy?'

'Of course. Part of Steve's pleasure came from making certain his impoverished cousins knew all about this.'

'Do you know exactly how rich he was?'

'How could I?'

'His total estate is approximately eight hundred and twenty-five thousand pounds.'

'Good God! I'd no idea it was of that order. Over three-quarters of a million! You don't need to worry about rates and a mortgage with that sort of money, do you? But maybe then you worry yourself sick about keeping it. I hope so. I'd like to think that the rich don't get off scot free.'

'He didn't,' said the DC.

'No, of course not . . . Edith's always telling me that my tongue is sharper than my brain.'

'Señor,' said Alvarez, 'do you know who inherits his estate?'

'I haven't the slightest idea, beyond the fact that it won't be me.'

'In his will, practically everything is left to his brother.'

'That's fair enough. Amelia always said that although he was stupidly pompous to Alan, and Alan deliberately annoyed him, at heart they got on well together.'

'However, under a will which was not executed, his estate was to go to his future wife.'

'That's to be expected.'

'You knew he intended to marry again?'

'Amelia told me that it was in the offing. To some socialite whose only interest in life is horses. Her attraction was her title and her entrée into high places And that makes him pathetic and not just plain nasty.'

'You consider he was a nasty person?'

'I know all about *de mortuis nil nisi bonum*, but I've never believed that death sanctified anyone. Steve behaved like a shit to Agnes—I met her a couple of times and quite liked her. Then she died and I never heard that he expressed one word of regret at her death. All he was interested in was how wealthy he now was. You know, when you see someone like him receiving so much, it begins to make you realize that there's virtue in vice.'

'Steven Cullom was almost certainly murdered for his money.'

'So that means . . . You're really saying that Alan did it?'

'Why do you think that?'

'Well, it's obvious. First you tell me Alan inherits everything, then that Steve was killed for his money.'

'The one does not necessarily follow the other. Under the law in this country—and it is the same in mine—a man may not make money out of his crime. So if Alan Cullom is convicted of murdering his brother, he will not be allowed to inherit the money. Do you know who then would?'

'No.'

'His cousins.'

Ackroyd stared at him. 'His . . . his cousins? You mean . . . Are you saying it could be Amelia and me?'

'If he is convicted, yes. But that, of course, is quite different from saying, if he murdered him.'

'I don't understand.'

'Originally, there were three cousins who might have benefitted—yourself, Basil Cullom, and Amelia Hart. Last year, Basil Cullom died in a car accident. This year, Amelia Hart could so easily have died in another car accident. Then both of them would have died before Steven Cullom and so they would not have inherited.'

For a moment, Ackroyd failed to appreciate the full significance of what had just been said. Then his face flushed and he spoke with sharp anger. 'You're not trying to suggest I know anything about the murder of Steven?'

'If Amelia Hart had died earlier this year, you would have been the sole survivor who could inherit.'

'You can't make bloody stupid accusations like that.'

'Where were you on the night of the second of June?'

He struggled to calm his emotions sufficiently to think clearly. Finally, he said: 'I was staying with Amelia.'

'At what time did you go to bed?'

'How d'you expect me to be able to answer a question like that?'

'I suggest you try.'

'I just don't know. I can't place which day of the holiday it was. But all the time I was there, she never went out at night because she preferred not to.'

'And you?'

'I stayed in, of course, to be company for her. That was partially why I was invited.'

'Did you ever leave the house after the señora had gone to bed?'

'No.'

'Can you prove you didn't?'

'Has anyone ever pointed out to you that it's near impossible to prove a negative?'

'The señora might have come into your room or you have gone into hers?'

'Are you trying to suggest . . . '

'I'm asking if you think that the señora could vouch for the fact that on at least one evening you were in the house after she'd gone to bed.'

'I'm quite certain she couldn't.'

'Where were you at the beginning of March of last year?'

'Why d'you want to know that?'

'Basil Cullom's accident occurred on the third of March. Did you travel to Cumberland and sabotage his car so that it crashed and killed him?'

'Of course I bloody well didn't.'

'Where were you on the first, second, and third of that month?'

'Here. In my own home.'

'Can you prove that?'

Ackroyd stared bitterly at Alvarez, then left the room. When he returned, his wife was with him. She said, her voice hard, her expression angry: 'I don't understand how you can make such filthy accusations. If you can't realize that Maurice wouldn't hurt anyone, I'm very, very sorry for you.' She stopped. The silence lengthened. 'Can't you say something?'

'Señora, I am truly sorry, but I have to investigate the facts,' replied Alvarez.

'And that means calling innocent people murderers? You may be allowed to do that sort of thing in your country, but you're not in this. If there's any more, I'm going to get on to our solicitor.'

'Please, I know how terrible it is for you; believe me, I hate causing you so much distress. But I have to discover who did murder Steven Cullom.'

She was set off balance by his obvious and genuine sympathy. Her belligerence changed to bewilderment. 'But you can't think Maurice would do such a terrible thing.'

'Can you tell us where your husband was on the first three days of March of last year?'

She squared her shoulders. 'On the first we were here, together, on the second we went out in the evening to a meal because it was my birthday, on the third we were here.'

'Señora, do you have a passport?'

'Yes.'

'May I see it, please?'

'Why?' demanded Ackroyd.

'It will have the date of the señora's birthday.'

He looked at his wife; she stared back with hopeless fear.

'Well, how about getting it, then?' said the DC sharply.

'My birthday's not then,' she said, in little more than a whisper. 'But he was here, all the time; he must have been. We can't afford to go out. The only time he's away is when we all go camping or when Amelia's asked him.'

Alvarez stood. 'Thank you for all your help, señora.'

Her voice rose again. 'You don't believe me. You don't understand that he couldn't . . .' She came to a stop, accepting that repetition would not ensure belief.

Alvarez said in Spanish: 'If I need to question you again, I'll come back.'

Ackroyd replied in English: 'I've told you all I know.'

When the two detectives were seated in the car, Mather said, as he started the engine: 'What's the form now? Presumably you'll ask us to arrest him and you'll start extradition proceedings? I don't imagine we'll get anywhere now with that crash up in Cumberland unless, of course, he makes a confession.'

'First,' replied Alvarez, 'I think I must return to Mallorca and ask Señora Amelia Hart a few more questions, just to make absolutely certain.'

Mather drew out from the pavement. 'It's no fun, is it? Going into a house like that, wife, kids, everything reasonably happy, and knowing you're going to smash it all to pieces. Our job can be a real sod.'

Alvarez nodded.

CHAPTER 23

On Thursday night an airliner crashed in Peru, killing all the passengers and crew; in consequence of this, by Friday morning Dolores had tearfully buried Alvarez, even before his plane took off from Heathrow. So when he walked into the house in time for a late lunch, she greeted him with the fevered emotion to be expected on his return from the grave. It was quite some time—she'd been given her present and had been persuaded to drink a calming brandy—before she regained her normal poise.

'I have prepared a special meal,' she announced, overlooking the fact that had he died he would have been unable to enjoy it.

He sniffed the air. 'It's not . . .?'

'Lechona.'

'If you'd asked me to choose, I'd have answered lechona, tasting of spicy heaven and with crackling to melt in the mouth.'

She was well satisfied. 'Good. And there's time for another drink before I serve.'

Jaime grabbed the bottle of brandy and refilled his glass. It was a long time since she had suggested he had another drink.

Ca'n Oñar came into sight. So beautiful, he thought . . . He parked, walked up to the front door, and knocked. After a minute, Hart opened the door. 'You've really caught us on the hop! For once we had a late night listening to the radio, and this morning we decided to allow ourselves that most sybaritic of all pleasures, breakfast in bed. So we were only just getting up when you arrived. Which goes to show that self-indulgence never pays.'

'I am sorry to be too early.'

'It's after ten and yet you can honestly talk about its being too early! That's one of the things I admire so much about this island . . . Would you like a coffee?'

'There is no need . . .'

'We'd like some more, anyway. Make yourself at home. Amelia will be out in a jiffy.'

Alvarez sat. A humming-bird hawk-moth began to work a deep red rose, just beyond the edge of the patio, and he watched it as it searched for nectar. A cicada started shrilling, stopped, started again. A quick movement on the nearest pillar caught his attention and he saw a gecko making its quick, wiggle-woggle way up to the top and then pass out of sight along the cross-beam . . .

Amelia came out on to the patio in her wheelchair. 'Pat says he's already apologized for our terrible slackness, so I won't . . . And please sit down again.'

She settled the wheelchair on the far side of the table to him. 'Well, what's brought you this time? Something fresh?'

Before he could answer, Hart came out with a tray on which were three cups of coffee, milk, and sugar. As he passed the coffee round, she said: 'Have you come to tell us that after all, Steve died in an accident?'

'No, señora. He was murdered.'

'Oh! I was hoping . . . It's all so horrible.'

'Yes,' agreed Hart, 'in spite of the fact that he was the kind of man he was.'

'What difference does that make?'

'There's less horror in a sinner being murdered than a saint.'

'There isn't. It's the murder that's so awful and that doesn't depend at all on the victim.'

'So the murder of a sadistic torturer is no less heinous an offence than the murder of someone who's never done anything but good?'

'The act of murder is the same. It's the consequences which are different. And in any case, it's unfair to choose such extremes.'

'On the contrary, you can always test the logic of an argument by taking it to extremes.'

'Very Humpty Dumpty. When you say logic, the word means what you want it to mean.' She smiled. 'Poor Inspector! You must think we spend our days squabbling?'

'I'm sure he can differentiate between an intelligent discussion and a squabble,' said Hart. 'And incidentally, you'll find that as a policeman he agrees with me.'

She turned. 'Well—do you?'

'No, señora, I agree with you. Murder is always horrible because it affects so many—the murderer, the victim, and the innocent.'

'I think that's a slightly different viewpoint from mine. But so very true. Perhaps it's enough to say it's horrible and not to search out why.' She spooned some sugar into her coffee. 'I shouldn't be having this—but I couldn't face tea and lemon. Why are so many of our pleasures forbidden fruit?'

'That's obvious,' said Hart. 'To make them pleasurable.'

'I could discuss that at some length, but with lots of sympathy for our guest, I'm not going to . . .' She faced Alvarez once more. 'You haven't had the chance to tell us what you've found out now?'

'I can be certain at last what was the motive for the murder.'

'What was it?'

'Señor Steven Cullom's fortune.'

'And that goes to Alan . . . So you're saying he murdered Steven?' asked Hart.

'No, señor. Under British law, he is not allowed to inherit if he committed the murder. In such a case, it will be as if Steven Cullom died intestate. Because all more immediate relatives are dead, his cousins would inherit.'

'Are you saying . . . that Maurice and Amelia . . .?'

'I said that was so if he were convicted of murdering his brother.'

'Good God! . . . And will he be convicted?'

'No, I don't think so. You see, he did not kill his brother. Someone else committed the murder, set the scene to make it appear it had been Alan. That way, Alan would not be allowed to inherit the estate he had been left in the will.'

'Who's this someone else?'

'Is that not obvious? It has to be whoever inherits if Alan does not.'

'But that's saying . . . Either Maurice or my wife is the murderer.'

Amelia's anger was immediate. 'How dare you come here and make such an absurd and disgusting allegation.'

'Señora, I am afraid there is truth in it.'

'You can't mean Maurice . . .'

'I have been in England, to question Señor Ackroyd. He was staying here with you on the night of the murder. His cousin was probably killed between two and four in the morning of the Friday. Can you say whether he was in the house at that time?'

'But . . . but how can I say something like that? I must
have gone to bed early because I always do—except occasionally, like last night. I often take a sleeping pill, so I
sleep rather heavily. And even if I didn't that night, I
wouldn't have dreamt of going into his bedroom . . . I
couldn't even have gone into it if I'd wanted. I sleep downstairs. He slept upstairs. And he wouldn't have dreamed of
coming into my room unless there'd been an emergency.'

'If he'd taken the car, would you have been disturbed
when it was started up and driven away?'

'I . . . Yes, I'm certain I would have been.'

'You are quite sure, señora?'

She hesitated, then shook her head. 'I suppose I've got
to be honest. It would have taken more than that to get
through to me . . . But it couldn't have been Maurice.'

Alvarez spoke to Hart. 'You were in England?'

'That's right.'

'Can you prove that you were there on the night of
Thursday, the second of this month?'

'Why should I try?'

'I have to make certain of all the facts in this very sad
case. I think that in English you have the expression, "to
tie up all the loose ends".'

'I still don't see that it matters a fig where I was.'

'You are the husband of one of the two surviving cousins
—I am forgetting Alan Cullom for a moment. It will be best
if I can say with complete certainty where you were, since
that will negate one possibility.'

'What possibility?'

'The allegation that you committed the murder after
flying out to this island for a few hours.'

'Who the hell's suggested anything that fantastic? Is that
what Maurice did?'

'Perhaps you would tell me if you can confirm that you
didn't fly here that night? I much regret having to ask, but
it is my duty.'

'Duty be . . .'

Amelia interrupted. 'Pat, the inspector has to do his duty.'

' "Thank God, I have done my duty." . . . All right. But I don't suppose I can prove any such thing. I stayed with the Spencers on the first of the month. I know that much. They lent me the car to go on up to the Yeats near Newcastle. But I didn't want to go that far in one go . . . That's right, I stayed the night in a motel close to Nottingham.'

'Then someone at the motel would have seen you during the evening?' asked Alvarez.

'Well, I don't know about that. I arrived earlier than I'd expected and booked in and had to pay in advance. And from then on, I don't believe I saw any of the staff. Like so many places these days, it was all self-service; make your own morning tea, polish your own shoes, and, since you've paid in advance, clear off when you feel like it.'

'But wasn't that the night when you went to the theatre?' she asked.

'Was it? . . . Well, I suppose it must have been since I wasn't anywhere near Nottingham at any other time.'

'You brought me back the programme and the ticket stub, knowing how I'd sentimentally remember when we went to *West Side Story* in London . . .' She turned to Alvarez. 'I suppose you want to see them to make certain I'm telling the truth?' She tried to speak lightly, but failed. Her husband had been doubted and so she was like a vixen defending its young.

Alvarez shook his head. 'Señora, I could not doubt your word.' He paused, then said: 'I now have only one more question. Do you know how Steven Cullom's dog acted towards Alan Cullom?'

'All I can tell you is that Steve once said to me that it couldn't stand Alan.'

Alvarez stood. 'Señor, may I trouble you a little more? Will you come to the guardia post in Llueso and sign a statement, detailing what you have just told me?'

'Of course.' Hart came to his feet. 'It was Maurice, then?'

'It couldn't have been either of them,' said Amelia angrily.

Hart put a hand on her arm as it rested on the chair. 'You're right, of course . . . I won't be long. But I will just nip down to the port afterwards and see if I can buy a newspaper.'

They drove away in two cars. They parked beyond the bus station and then walked, for the most part in silence, to the guardia post.

In his office, Alvarez opened the shutters to let the sunshine stream in. He set a chair before the desk and they both sat.

'If you could prepare the statement for me to sign?' said Hart. 'We had thought of going out for a picnic. It does Amelia a world of good to get away from the house.'

Alvarez said in Spanish: 'To which part of the island will you go for your picnic?'

Hart said in English: 'I'm sorry, but I don't know what you're on about. My Spanish is limited to "red wine, please" and I always hope the waiter doesn't bring the tomato ketchup.'

'Then you are not certain what the Spanish for child is?'

'I'm not, no. But I don't suppose that's important and if I'm to get a newspaper first I am a bit pressed . . .'

'On the contrary, it matters a great deal that you don't immediately know that the word *niño* has a tilde. Just as it matters a great deal that you have an alibi for the evening of the second of this month and Maurice Ackroyd does not. It makes it certain that it is you who murdered Steven Cullom.'

'I what? For Christ's sake! If I've got an alibi, it means I couldn't have done.'

'If the alibi could be checked in every detail, of course. But on your own admission, it can't. You could have bought the ticket to the theatre and a programme and yet never have attended the performance. You admit that no one at the hotel can vouch for you . . . Only the murderer knew that he might need an alibi and therefore set out to provide himself with as good a one as he could.'

'This is bloody nonsense.'

'Sadly, it is the truth.'

'I don't have to stay here and listen . . .'

'You do,' said Alvarez, and his voice was now thick with contempt. 'For a time I could not understand why the dog's throat had been cut. Then I saw that this barbarism might have been committed by someone with a special reason to hate the dog and who, in a perverted sense, was thus getting his own back. Alan Cullom had tried to be friendly with it, but his brother had egged on the dog to dislike him. So Alan could have had reason to hate it. But he didn't; he went on trying to make friends. Yet someone who had never seen him with the dog and who had only heard about the relationship from a third person might well believe that he did hate it and would have reason to vent his hatred.

'Steven Cullom told your wife that the dog hated Alan and, I imagine, that this infuriated Alan. She told you this. Just as she told you about Beatriz. Señor Ackroyd could only have known about Beatriz if your wife had also told him, but she is a woman who never gossips even to a cousin; a husband, naturally, is different.'

'You're crazy! Are you forgetting that in February we damn near crashed and you suggested the brakes had deliberately been tampered with. If someone was trying . . . '

'It was you who tampered with the brakes, relying on your skill as a driver to avoid an accident when the brakes failed.'

'I'd have to be mad to take that sort of a risk.'

'Or very sane and clever. There were five cousins, in four families. Their parents had hated each other and in only one case were those hates not passed on. Whatever your feelings were as the husband of the one cousin who didn't hate, when you were made redundant by a firm for which you'd worked for years, and when you saw Steven Cullom, whom you'd always despised, inherit a fortune and become rich almost beyond imagination, you grew so jealous and so bitter that his weakness should be rewarded while your strength had been penalized, you learned to hate him as your wife could not.

'Then Steven Cullom, who liked your wife, invited you both out here for the first time, two years ago. He lent you a house and a car, he paid the wages of the part-time staff. Sometimes, there is nothing that so exacerbates a hatred as generosity. That was the time when you worked out how to murder him and benefit from the murder. And because you were intelligent, you schooled yourself to move slowly and to wait to carry out each step until the circumstances were wholly in your favour.

'Because Steven was so fond of your wife, he talked freely to her and she came to know many things about him. She told them to you. She didn't understand that you were noting everything and waiting for the right moment to murder him so that you, through her, would inherit part of his fortune.

'You set the murder to look as if a bungled attempt had been made to present the death as an accident. You made certain that the Bennassar brothers would come under suspicion. But you went on to arrange things so that it would become clear that they had not killed him out of revenge, he had been murdered by someone else from greed. And who would kill him except his brother who, under the existing will, inherited virtually everything? And if he were found guilty, the estate would be distributed among the cousins.

'Why did you not murder Maurice as well as Basil? Because you were sufficiently intelligent to realize that your plan, however cleverly worked out, might just go wrong and it might become clear that Alan had not been the murderer. So you added yet another layer of deceit. If the finger of suspicion was ever pointed not at Alan, but at a cousin, it must settle on Maurice—which is why he was invited here when you were in England.'

'That's all balls.'

'Those are the facts.'

'If Steve was murdered for his money, Alan murdered him, never expecting to lose the inheritance through being found guilty.'

'There is no proof of that.'

'There goddamn well is. Only you're so incompetent you haven't found it.'

'Then tell me what it is and compensate for my incompetence.'

Hart, about to answer heatedly, stopped himself. Just in time he remembered that if Alvarez didn't know there was a letter in the Santa Victoria post office, addressed to Alan Ernest, containing the missing draft will, then it was impossible to acquaint him of the fact without admitting to being the murderer . . . Equally, to draw attention to the yachting plimsolls, carefully impressed with soil from around the body . . .

Alvarez came to his feet, went round the desk and over to the window. He stared out at the sun-sodden street. 'Life is so often sad and cruel. Sad because once something is done, it cannot be undone; cruel because a guilty person can seldom be made to suffer without also hurting an innocent one. That is why punishment can seldom be just.

'Basil Cullom is dead and nothing can bring him back to life; your conviction for his murder cannot restore the tears to his widow. Steven Cullom is dead; he deserved to die, but not to be murdered. Not because that was too brutal; but because murder can never be committed in isolation.'

Alvarez turned round. 'If you are charged with murder, you will be found guilty. When found guilty, you will be imprisoned. But then your wife will suffer still further: surely she has already suffered more than enough? And she is innocent of anything but too much love and trust. Two lives destroyed when only one should be forfeit.

'Yet if you are not imprisoned, will you escape all penalties for two murders and for destroying the happiness of Edith Cullom?' He slowly shook his head. 'We all can carry hell around inside us. You will find your hell knowing that because of what you did, Alan is rich while you remain poor.'

'What's that?' Salas demanded over the telephone.

'Señor,' replied Alvarez, 'I am now convinced that unless fresh evidence ever comes to light, it will be impossible to finally decide who killed Steven Cullom.'

'What about those shoes?'

'Although they are Alan Cullom's, there can be no proof that he was wearing them when the earth was gathered up.'

'Surely you learned something from your trip to England?'

'Only, señor, that, as I've just said, lacking any vital and exclusive piece of evidence, it is impossible to name the murderer.'

'Are you confessing that you've buggered up this case the same as all the others?'

'Yes, señor.'

'At least you're consistent, aren't you?'

Alvarez parked in front of Ca'n Cullom and crossed to the front door, rang the bell. María answered the call and led him through to the pool patio where both Susan and Alan Cullom were sunbathing.

'I've been making further investigations and thought you should know the results,' he said.

'Well?' Alan Cullom's face reflected the strain under which he'd been living.

'It will be held that your brother was killed by person or persons unknown.'

'But . . . Are you saying . . . You told me that letter in

the post office made it obvious I was guilty,' said Alan
Cullom.

'I don't think I said more than that it appeared to make
it obvious.'

'But you were wrong?'

'Not really. It's just that I forgot to mention it to my
superior. He knows nothing about it.'

Alan Cullom stared at him, bewildered.

'Why haven't you told him?' asked Susan.

He wanted to answer that originally it had been because
of a pair of deep blue eyes in which a man could drown even
before he realized he was in danger; but he said, 'Señorita,
I am not clever and so there are very many things I do not
understand. Why should the innocent suffer as well as the
guilty, why should happiness be taken away from someone
who has already lost so much?'

'Does that mean you're not ever going to tell anyone
about the letter?'

'I am not, no. And in return I would ask two small
favours.'

'Two small favours?' repeated Alan slowly. His voice
sharpened. 'You know what this is, Susan, don't you? A
shakedown.'

'How can you be so stupidly blind?' she cried in exasperation. 'Can't you begin to understand people? If the inspector
truly thought you were guilty, you could offer him the world
and he'd refuse it.'

'Maybe. Maybe not.' He said to Alvarez: 'So just what
are the two "small favours"?'

'If you are not found guilty of the murder of your brother,
you will be a rich man.'

'So it hasn't taken long to get round to money after all.'

'Señor, many people have been hurt by your brother, but
I only know of two who can be compensated. One was hurt
because he lived, one because he died. Beatriz will be having
his baby. She has a job now, but soon she will have to leave

it. Her family are not well off and it would be nice for her not to have to worry about extra expenses.

'Lady Molton had a dream. When your brother was killed, her dream also died. You could restore that dream to her. Lend her enough money to continue with her horses.'

Susan stood and crossed to where he sat. She took hold of his right hand in both of hers. 'I wish . . . How I wish you had a dream we could give you.'

He stared out at the land and marvelled at the unthinking cruelty of youth.